I0831921

THE VISITOR

TENTH ANNIVERSARY EDITION

K P WEAVER

First published 2012
This edition published in 2022 by MMH Press, Waikiki, WA 6169

This is a work of fiction. All of the characters, names, incidents, organisations and dialogue in this novel are either the products of the author's imagination or are used fictitiously.

Because of the dynamic nature of the Internet, any web addresses or links contained in this book may have changed since publication and may no longer be valid. The views expressed in this work are solely those of the author and do not necessarily reflect the views of the publisher and the publisher hereby disclaims any responsibility for them.

The intent of the author is only to offer information of a general nature to help you in your quest for emotional and spiritual wellbeing. In the event you use any of the information in this book for yourself, which is your constitutional right, the author and the publisher assume no responsibility for your actions.

Edited by Teena Raffa-Mulligan

A catalogue record for this work is available from the National Library of Australia

National Library of Australia Catalogue-in-Publication data:

ISBN:
978-0-6455205-5-2
(Harback)

978-0-6455205-4-5
(Paperback)

978-0-6455205-6-9
(Ebook)

For my wonderful gifts,
Dylan, Eithen, Kiera, Saoirse, Eimear and Mary,
I am complete because of you.

From all negative situations
is the potential for a positive outcome.
Karen P Weaver

Introduction

My 'Visitor' Journey

Little did I know, that at the end of October 2008, I would have an inspired thought, an epiphany that would change the entire trajectory of my life. I was a mum of four at the time, and an Irish immigrant, having just moved to Perth. I was happy in my new life, content to be a mum at home with my kids, my youngest being just four weeks old at the time.

I was learning and growing, in fact, I was having a spiritual journey, so things were interesting.

I was just doing what I *felt* I needed to do for every next step. With three of my kids under five, one being a new baby, I generally had ABC Kids on TV in the morning, but for some reason, one morning, I found myself watching *The View*. We never had day-time TV on in our house, apart from this day, but that's when my epiphany came to me. Whoopi Goldberg was on *The View* with a celebrity couple who were being interviewed after having recently experienced a miscarriage. They were a well-known couple who had their own reality TV show, so everybody knew about their recent trauma, and it was very obvious that the woman was still very distraught. I absolutely connected, as I had been through a miscarriage too, and it was then I received a message that *I just had to* write about my experience.

In that moment, my heart connected with her heart and I felt everything she was feeling. I could feel her wondering, *Why me? I really loved and wanted this baby. Why did I lose it?* We connected so strongly, because in December 2007, that was me. I'd had a traumatising double miscarriage and I remembered feeling all those things, just wanting to be full again.

The year before my double miscarriage had been a year like no other. I experienced PTSD after my brother and partner had a very serious fight. What I remember from that was that I felt like I left my body and was energetically 'beside' myself, from the outside looking in, and I'll never forget that feeling. When you go through PTSD, you're just living through the motions of each day. You don't really 'feel' anything, you're quite numb to things.

But about sixteen months later, I discovered I was pregnant.

It was a surprise as we weren't really trying, but it was a welcome surprise – one that filled me full of hope.

This gave me the spark I needed to move forward and let me back inside my heart, body and mind. I was so happy that I could feel something again. But after a few days of getting used to our new-found happiness, we went to an event, and the next morning, I woke up and had started bleeding.

It was just a little spot at first, but it wasn't long before I knew I had lost my baby. We went to the hospital and did a scan, and to my surprise, there was still a heartbeat. There was another baby, and it was fine, and it was strong. I remember feeling all sorts of emotions; sad for the baby I had lost, but elated and hopeful for the baby still growing within me.

My sister had also been a twin, so I held on to the hope that my baby would be healthy and prayed to my granny to please let this baby live. As I was lying there, I remember the moment that it 'popped' and I knew I had now lost both my babies. My heart broke.

It was in that moment that I cried. I cried tears until I was empty. Tears and tears and tears for the babies and for the year and a half I'd lost beforehand. The release was intense and the overwhelming emotions so different from the numbness I had felt for so long.

When I went back to the hospital after having the miscarriage, I was practically told, 'It happens all the time. You've got two healthy boys. Just get over it and get on with life.'

But when your heart aches, and physically hurts in your grief, you can't just 'get over' something. I had wanted them so much but it wasn't to be. However, I realised the pregnancy had brought me back to life, after my year of PTSD. We decided to try for another baby. I was very blessed, got pregnant straightaway and had my rainbow baby. And then, two-and-a-half years and another baby later, I found myself in Australia in the middle of a moment of epiphany, watching *The View* on TV.

Whoopi Goldberg turned to the reality TV star who had just experienced a miscarriage, and she said, 'When it's an early miscarriage, and I must stress *early miscarriage,* I want to tell you something that I tell all my friends this happens to: this was a visitor that came down to tell you to be ready and get back on the right path, as that is when your true gift will come.' Those words hit me like a lightning bolt.

I connected with those words so deeply because I understood why, on a spiritual level, I had endured a miscarriage. I had been too long in PTSD. I was on the wrong path. Everything was going wrong in my life. And yet, when I had the miscarriage and then the subsequent pregnancy, everything started to go right – I could feel again. Okay, they weren't the greatest feelings, because I was sad, but at least I was feeling something.

I understood what Whoopi was talking about because when I got back on the right path, life improved. We ended up getting married, we got our visas for Australia and we moved to Perth, all within one year. So many amazing things started to flow. I was writing articles for a website, and they were getting quite a bit of traction at the time, but I knew there was more for me.

One day, I discovered that in two day's time, NaNoWriMo (National Novel Writing Month) was happening. And suddenly, I had a calling to write a novel. I knew this would be difficult with a four-week-old baby, but the call was too large to ignore. I told my husband, 'I'm sorry – you don't have a wife for a month. I'm going to write 1,667 words every day of the month.' I had worked out the number of words I needed to write daily to produce a fifty-thousand-word novel in just one month!

So I did it, every single day. I showed up, and *The Visitor* was born. I wrote the title in the middle of the page, circled it and gave each of the characters scenarios. I wrote down twenty possible chapters and then … just started writing. And I allowed one of the characters to be me!

It was amazing how the characters took on a life of their own. I didn't know what was going to happen when I wrote it, but it ended up being published and getting really good rewiews. I had no idea what the publishing process would look like, so I really went on a journey. It was a bit daunting and definitely an education. To be honest, the publishing process was quite a negative experience, but

I really did learn a lot.

Then later, when someone asked me if I could help publish *their* book, I was like, 'You know what, I probably could.'

So I did some research into the print and distribution channel my publisher in the US had used, and I discovered they had opened up an office in Melbourne. I made a sacred promise to myself that should I apply to become a publisher, and if accepted, I would help other authors tell their stories and help them to have a more positive experience. And I have been showing up for that every day since. That was ten years ago now, and I never, ever regret it.

So my novel, *The Visitor*, was the first book I ever wrote. I believe it was the best book I've ever written, and I'm so glad I did it. And when people read it and get the wisdom that's in it, magic happens. I will never, ever forget the first time I was told that reading the book had changed their life.

The book leads people to the answers their heart longs for, even if that might just be to understand their true grief. There's an important message in this book for people who are grieving, as well as those who need words of comfort and understanding around their grief.

When you have an impact like that through your words, you become very purposeful in your actions. The calling was so very loud that I have continued to show up for authors and their stories ever since. Part of the journey of *The Visitor* was that it was my catalyst into publishing. Without it, I would never have been inspired to build a million-dollar publishing press, while being an at-home mum to now six kids. Without it, I would never have been able to have the wonderful experiences I've had working with some amazing people. I wouldn't have been able to inspire others every day.

It's humbling to think of the many marvellous books that may never have been published had I not had the courage to take action and actually sit down and write *The Visitor*. Because I said 'hell yes!' to this book coming to be, so many unexpected events have turned my life into a fantastic journey.

It's just so important to show up for yourself, even when it seems irrational. Well, especially if it seems irrational, that's when it's probably the right thing for you, because it's so different than what everyone else is doing. When you have the courage to step outside your comfort zone, away from the crowd, you can enjoy the experience so much more – in fact, you will find out what the true magic of life is. I've learned so much on my writing and publishing journey and I wouldn't change a moment of it.

On the tenth anniversary of the release of my first novel, I thank you for joining me on the journey of *The Visitor*. It's incredible to think of what has been achieved in ten years. I still love this book so much, and I hope that you love it too.

Prologue

There is a special place, somewhere in the Heavenly universe. You may already feel this place does exist; yet you will never truly know of its existence unless you have experienced the magic it delivers directly to those chosen few who are its receivers. It is from this place that this journey began.

Five special, but significantly different, women became eligible to experience the magic of changing their lives to receive the true gift. Because of what they know now, they will no longer see things in the same way, because I have a job to do. This is not a pleasant encounter at times. But in order for the true magnificence of my role to shine through the darkness, I must first endure a tough journey, and so must they.

The women came from across the globe, but their varied locations were never significant, as they are now joined by a bond deeper than most; some may never meet, but they will be connected forever through the memories I now hold.

Chapter One

The Meeting

I still do not fully understand why the Boss gave me this role and wonder what he saw in me to make him think I am the best person for the job. He must value my opinion highly to give me control of such a life-changing responsibility. No pressure, then! Right. But then again, perhaps not. My mates have started to call me 'the Indian', because I give a gift and then take it away. It's alright for them, with their conventional 'giving' jobs. Not so for me. The official name for my job is 'Visitor', the definition of which is 'a person or thing that enters into someone's life for a short time'. I am back after a break between assignments. Each assignment can take a lot out of me. The pressure can be intense, and I never know what to expect. Every assignment is different, from start to finish, so anything can happen.

Ah, Jonnie has sent me a message: *Meeting 10 mins boardroom.*

That means it's time. Soon, I will find out the identities of the people I'll spend the next few months with. I always feel nervous and a little uncomfortable at this point so I must remember to make a stop at the loo on the way to the meeting. The Boss doesn't like it if we need to leave the room, and sometimes these meetings can go on for hours.

My good friend, Sydney, had been out for a curry and a few glasses of wine the night before the last meeting, and they were doing a conga in her lower intestines the whole way through it. The sweat on her forehead and the greenness of her cheeks told a story of their own. The poor girl was in pain, but I have to commend her. She stuck it out until the end. Mind you, we didn't see her the rest of the afternoon, even though we usually hang out to make sure we are all in sync when the Boss isn't around.

Outside the boardroom door, we all line up in anticipation, as if we are waiting at the living room door to see what Santa left for us. As we look in through the small window in the door, the room is spacious, bright and airy. The prominent colour is white – white walls, white table, enormous white fluffy chairs – not the usual decor for a boardroom.

Sitting in those chairs is like lying on a giant cloud. When you sink in, it feels quite luxurious. But they are awkward to get out of, and I have not worked out why. It is all very strange, as this room is not one you would expect the Boss to have had an influence in designing, yet apparently it was his vision. Boss is quite loud and sharp; when he talks he has everyone's attention. Quite a bulky, strong man, nothing like me – I could fit twice into his pants. He has the utmost respect from everyone. No-one has ever questioned his decisions, as he has never faltered. I would trust him with my life. I suppose, in a way, I have.

We hear a loud, 'Come in!' so we all enter the room and take our seats at the large white desk, where our assignment files await us. I am dying to take a peek, but I decide to wait until it is time to read about the people I am going to encounter. I love meeting new people, delving into the soul of their lives in order to find their true being. What makes them tick? Do they already know, or will they find out in the future? Human behaviour has always intrigued me.

Boss gives us all the usual spiel: start afresh, forget the past assignments, take a fresh approach – all the usual get-in-the-zone focus stuff that helps us build a brick wall between assignments. And then comes the moment we are all awaiting.

'Well, what are you all waiting for? Open your files. Have a look, and if you have any questions that I can help you with before the end of the meeting, all the better. If not, you can take your time to look over them tonight, and be at my office early, because dispatch starts at nine o'clock sharp. Got it?' says Boss.

While we all reach for our files, we agree in unison,'Got it, Boss.'

On this assignment I have five different candidates to observe, and five special gems to pick up in the morning before I dispatch. The gems are not designed to last long, but they will have an unimaginable effect on those who encounter them. It never ceases to amaze me how everyone deals with these situations in their own unique way. Over the thirty-four years I have had this role, I believe I have seen it all – but, hey, maybe not. I never take things for granted; definitely not here, anyway. Once I have done my duty, I am not allowed to interfere; I must only observe for the immediate reaction and then report my findings to Boss and the others.

I am always asked how I am able to do my job. Well, someone has to do it, and I believe I do it properly by ensuring that, although the gift I deliver is taken away, there are only so many gifts to give, and I help in the process of choosing the best candidates in each assignment group.

Scanning my files, I see my first candidate is a thirty-year-old, blonde, blue-eyed woman named Carrie. As I look at her picture, I see her sparkle is hidden behind a dark cloud. Her profile says she had always lived life to the fullest until having her first child, which was when her partner encouraged her to give up her work and studies to focus on her family commitments. She has applied for a visa to move to the other side of the world, far away from her friends and family, to focus on the family unit she is creating with her partner.

All of this, and yet she hasn't considered having any more children! I am intrigued to know why. I delve further into her profile. Ah! Now I see the reason. About a year ago, a violent attack inside her home traumatised her and she suffered the symptoms of post-traumatic stress, which she is still trying to overcome. I try not to judge others, as it is by means of a combination of different circumstances that we each make dramatic choices. A lot more to discover here, I imagine.

Next is a thirty-eight-year-old woman named Tracy. Based on her appearance, she has had a rough life and has let herself go somewhat. It is amazing how the pressures of life can really reflect on someone's face. She has short brown hair and is wearing jeans that are too tight for her, which creates a muffin-top effect around her waist. Let's see what her profile says. Oh, she has a medical condition which she has not discovered yet. A miracle sent to her four years ago allowed her to conceive her son. She has been trying, to no avail, to have a second child, and she has had many miscarriages. She also takes care of her mum, who is not as mobile as she once was and thus needs a lot of care. Tracy's family has had its fair share of trauma, which has led her to become quite cautious and sometimes anxious. People perceive her as being a negative and dull person who often feels sorry for herself, regularly vocalising her sadness over losing another pregnancy.

Because some people can feel uncomfortable with the taboo subject of miscarriages, they avoid her. This leaves her feeling isolated, which only adds to her anxiety and paranoia, especially after a playgroup session. Again, I do not judge. I will take the time to encounter people for myself so I can understand the circumstances that have brought them to this place in life where they now stand.

The third candidate is a twenty-two-year-old model named Bethany. She is very beautiful, with long brown locks that flow elegantly over her slender shoulders. Her eyes are as brown as the darkest mocha, but she is so thin that her bones show through her tanned skin. Her profile says she has a boyfriend who is also famous. They are regular partygoers. Some in society have presumed they are together to get more publicity, as the paparazzi have followed their every move since their dating status became 'news'.

They seem to be what people perceive as a 'perfect couple' – if there is such a thing! She is Australian, he is American. What more could the world want than the hunky American actor and the glamorous Australian beauty? Ever since birth, Bethany has won every 'bonny baby' contest and beauty pageant available. Yet people have only seen her beautiful appearance, not who she is inside. But I can see she is in love, as she has a twinkle in her eye that is not love for herself. It is true love for her soulmate.

Again, I am intrigued to learn more about her life. My job becomes so much easier when I am interested in learning more.

Next is another thirty-eight-year-old woman. Kath looks a lot younger in her picture, which indicates a stress-free life; maybe she has not yet had children. She has a toned physique. Her hair is blonde and her eyes are blue. She seems to have a confident presence, which I can discern by her posture and facial expression. The profile says she has always been focused on her career and has always planned everything in her life in advance. Time has moved swiftly since Kath was in her twenties, and she has worked hard to become a highly successful fitness instructor. She appears regularly on daytime television and has produced numerous fitness videos.

She has had neither the time nor the space for children, as she storms through life at an ever-increasing pace, exercising and exercising and exercising some more. Kath is obviously very successful; but is she happy? That is what I would like to know. I read on to discover that, over the past few years, she has tried – unsuccessfully – to fall in love. Now she has started investigating a sperm donor, as she feels that is her only option; her biological clock ticks louder and louder, and she has not yet found the right person – the man she would love enough to partner with to create a family.

Many a debate goes on all over the world, through different lands, religions and cultures, about medical intervention when it comes to having children. Is it better to start a family when a woman is young and her body is in its prime? Or is it better for a woman to wait until she has secure job and is more mentally and emotionally prepared for raising a child responsibly? I still am out on this one. So many pros and cons exist for both; and from my experience, each individual is exactly that: individual, and therefore, having their own positives and negatives. We must always remember that no-one is perfect. However, being decent with some moral standards are preferred 'qualifications'.

The fifth and final file. This will be interesting; the Boss usually saves the best until last. Her photo shows a woman who takes care of herself. She is petite, with fiery red hair tied back tightly from her face. 'Let Your Hair Down Girl' comes to mind immediately. She has a killer instinct look in her eye. Not much softness here, and her choice of clothing is a business-like suit with killer heels – must be to match her killer look. I don't see a ring on her finger, and I suspect she doesn't know what is coming. Let's see what her profile reveals. Her name is Siobhan, she is thirty-four years old and has never wanted to get married or have children. Siobhan's sole focus in life has been to secure the top job at Maximus Corporations, a powerful law firm. There seems to be no limit to what moral hurdles she will jump to achieve that goal. I have no inkling at all as to how this is going to end up. However, I am intrigued to discover how this ambitious go-getter has arrived at this pinnacle.

'Rupert, are you still with us?' I hear Boss shouting in the distance.

Oh, that's me! 'Yeah, Boss. Sorry, I was just scanning my files.'

'I see that, Rupert, but what I want to know is if you have any questions to ask.'

'No, Boss. Everything seems to be in place.'

'All right. If that is all I can do for you all, I will get back to my office. I trust everything will run smoothly, then.' He intensely scans the room.

Everyone agrees and then we all exchange a look. We know the Boss has a lot of responsibility, but we all work voluntarily for this cause because we believe what we do is for the greater good of mankind. Do we look for anything in return? No. I suppose we do live comfortably when we are not on an assignment, but it is not as if we don't earn it.

There I go again. *Stop!* I tell myself. Where is my optimism? I do love it here – it is so Heavenly, and everyone is in the same boat, so we have a sense of camaraderie. Syd, Jonnie and I are good mates, and we help each other out a lot; our roles allow us to interact all the time, and people who have been through as much together as we have tend to get close to each other.

'Hey, Roo, what's up with you? You're off in a world of your own.'

'Sorry, Syd, you know me – just afloat in another thought bubble. What do you think of these assignments?'

'Yeah, pretty standard, really – well, apart from assignment five, of course; it will be interesting to see how that progresses. We will have to work closely on that one, I think. Are you okay about that one? She looks quite like …'

'Who? What do you mean, Syd?'

'No-one, Roo. You know me: I just jump to conclusions without any justification at times. Please don't pass any remarks. Do you fancy catching a coffee later?'

'Yeah, sounds great, Syd. Will need to be early, though. I want to get prepared for dispatch in the morning. You know I am always first to go.'

'Let's say six at my place this time? I'll pick up some Heavenly delights from Dave.'

'How can I resist such an offer? Are you gonna tell Jonnie, or will I?'

'He said to confirm a time via message. He has had to rush off to get some form signed by the Boss.'

'Oh shit! I need my dispatch form signed, too, otherwise I can't get the gems released. There is no way I am going running around in the morning.'

I quickly jump up, grab my files and run around to the other side of the desk, where Syd is trying to get out of her chair.

So I bend down, meeting her halfway to give her a friendly thank you kiss.

'Syd, what would I do without you?'

'But I just said … Oh, well, you're welcome, then,' she replies, as she tries to get up while watching me dash out the door.

Outside the door, I have the unfortunate encounter of bumping right into Jayden.

'Whoa, Rupert, you are in a hurry! Did you forget something important? Maybe you forgot to take back the gift you gave, Indian boy.'

I just ignore him, as I don't want to fuel the fire he is trying to ignite. I start to walk away, and he continues to shout after me, for all to hear.

'If you can't handle that job of yours I can always take it off your hands! Make sure you tell Boss that when he discovers how incompetent you can be.'

Oh,he does rag me sometimes, but he is just jealous. Although I understand that is where his fire is coming from, it doesn't justify how he expresses his frustration. But I know the day will come when he moves on, so I will bide my time until then. I stand glorious in the knowledge that I am what he wants to be, and it is he who has issues, not I.

I make it around to Boss' office in good time and knock lightly on the door.

'Come in, Rupert,' he calls loudly.

I hate it when he does that! He makes me feel that he knows my innermost thoughts.

'Take a seat. Would you like a drink?' he asks, while making himself an espresso in his fancy machine.

'No thanks, Boss. I am meeting Syd and Jonnie for a coffee later, and I don't want to overdo it. I will never sleep tonight!'

He takes a seat opposite me in his big, white-leather chair, which he fills completely – it would take four of me to fill it.

Keen to move on after a moment of awkward silence, he says, 'Have you got the dispatch form there, Rupert?'

'Oh, yes, the form. It's right here.' I fumble in my bag.

Ah, got it – thank goodness. As he signs the dispatch forms, he asks, 'Are you looking forward to this assignment, Rupert?'

'Yes, Boss. I will look over the files in more detail tonight, of course, but it all seems intriguing.'

'Case five has very close similarities to …'

'I know what you are going to say. And no, that is not a problem, Boss.'

'Remember the profile, Rupert, because what is inside is not the same.'

'Yes, Boss, and it is what's inside that matters the most. If that's all, Boss …'

'Yes, Rupert, that's all. I hope your dispatch goes smoothly, and I will check in with you at some stage.'

'I will look forward to that!' I say sarcastically, as I quickly move towards the door.

'Rupert!' I hear, just as I reach my exit. I roll my eyes and turn around to see the Boss with his hand raised high, holding up my signed dispatch form. He knows I've been distracted. There's no point in digging a bigger hole for myself, so I just grab it, smile my glowing smile and leave as quickly as possible.

Chapter Two

Dispatch

Syd's quarters are across the corridor. On her door she has a big diamond number eight, and she feels it is her destiny to live there, as that has always been her favourite lucky number. I am not a real believer in all that kind of stuff, but if it encourages positivity, what harm can it do? Especially for Syd, as she tends to imagine the worst-case scenario, even though she always has good intentions.

I close my white but nonetheless dull-looking number seven door, and then walk across the corridor to Syd's place. She must have a sensor on me, as she opens the door before I knock.

'Ah … great! Just in time, Jonnie is on his way. And Dave has just made his delivery; I think Jayden is onto our secret meeting. Apparently he asked Dave a lot of questions.'

'Jayden does have issues. You know that, Syd,' I say as I take a seat.

Inside is no less glitzy than her door. Diamonds and crystals on every wall, and a giant crystal Cupid statue sitting right in the middle of her glass-topped coffee table, which has legs shaped like

Roman pillars. I do not know why, but every time I go for a cuppa, Cupid is always pointing at me. Believe me, I avoid it! The last thing I need in my life is for Cupid's arrow to strike me. It struck me before, with detrimental effects on my behaviour because I totally devoted myself to, and sacrificed everything for, love. But let's be optimistic – at least there is a substantial plate of Dave's Heavenly delights beside the statue.

'Yeah, I know, Roo. What is the deal with you and him? Is he after your job? I always thought he was suited to the power he had as head of dispatch, but obviously not. I wonder what lengths he will go to. You may not be safe …'

'Oh, stop it, Syd! None of us can even go to the loo without the Boss knowing it. Let's be realistic; any issues Jayden has are his problem to solve, not mine. I have a very important assignment to focus on.'

'You're right, I know, but there is no harm in being cautious around Jayden, Roo – especially after dispatch. Boss can't watch everything then.'

'Alright. I promise I will be more aware. Now can we get into the coffee and Heavenly delights? I need a sugar rush.'

'We had better wait for Jonnie. You know what he is like if we start without him!'

'Well he had better be quick.'

'There he is now,' she said a full beat before we heard theknock on the door.

'How do you do that, Syd?'

She just gives me a cheeky smile as she gets up to answer the door.

Jonnie comes in, all apologetic – as usual. He will pass himself someday, if he hasn't already.

'Hi, Roo! Have you and Jayden been at it again? It's the talk of the lower domain.'

'What are you talking about, Jonnie?'

'The argument that you guys had in the big corridor after today's meeting.'

'Does an argument not need two people to participate?'

'Well, yes, I think so. What do you think, Syd?'

'I think it takes two to tango.'

'That doesn't help, Syd.'

'Well, if you don't like the answer, Jonnie, don't ask my opinion.'

'Okay, you two. See, that could be considered an argument. I didn't answer Jayden today, so I did not have an argument. Can we please get some coffee now, Syd?'

'Coming right up. Large, fluffy-dream espressos all around?'

Our eager nods show our delight in, and need for, caffeine. Syd is back in an instant, and all three of us are silent for a few moments as the espresso enters our caffeine-starved bodies. We all then indulge in a delicious Heavenly delight.

'Wow! I so miss these when I am away.' I lick the lightest, fluffiest cream from around my mouth and giggle when I notice that Syd, as always, has cream all over her nose and mouth. *Not gonna tell her, though*. From the smirk on Jonnie's face, I suspect he isn't either.

For the next hour we drink coffee, eat Heavenly delights, and go through each file – but there is only so much we can talk about without speculating. Our meetings are really a catch-up and support group for each other. So much can happen so quickly around here that it is good to have mates.

'I might head on now, I'll be getting up super early.'

'Yeah, I might go now as well, Syd. We'll let you hit the sack, too.'

'All right, guys. Great to catch up! We must not leave it as long next time.'

We wish each other well with our dispatches, and then Jonnie and I head back to our own quarters to wind down.

***

I don't sleep much. I never do the night before dispatch. It all seems so unnatural – I suppose it is, really; it is a process that was created. I never will fully understand it, and maybe I should look into it more. 'Knowledge is key', after all.

Anyway, I had better get up. I had set my alarm for six o'clock, which would have given me three hours to get ready, but I have already hit snooze a few times and now it is twenty-five past. I hop out of my bed, which is quite big and comfy. It is the main luxury I possess. I am not into clutter; I'm more minimalistic. I suppose you could call that my style. Keep things simple, because life is complicated enough at times.

Wiping the sleep from my eyes, I think about what lies ahead. I must keep a clear focus on the target destinations of my assignments. After showering and dressing, I read through the files once more and then head for the dispatch department.

When I arrive, there is a bit of a commotion. Jayden comes towards me in a determined manner.

'Where have you been? Your dispatch has been brought forward. Hurry up!'

'What? Why? What's going on? I haven't even collected the gems yet.'

'I have them ready for you here. Sign this and get going, or you will hold everyone else up.'

'But the Boss didn't inform me of any changes.'

'He did try to contact you last night, but you weren't in your quarters. As it was just a fifteen-minute change, and you are usually ready to dispatch early, he thought it wouldn't be a problem. Trust you to take your time this morning! You'd better hurry.'

'Oh, right, thanks. Will do.' I sign the form, take the wooden box containing the gems and head to the dispatch room as fast as I can. Something else must be happening today to cause such an upheaval. I am surprised that I wasn't told sooner. Boss is usually meticulous. Something doesn't feel right, so I call Syd on my way to hear what she thinks. I know she will imagine the worst-case scenario, but together we may come to some conclusion. I get no answer, so I send her a message:

Hi, Syd. Jayden acting strange @ dispatch – made rush through entry & pick-up. Call soon … Roo.

Maybe I am just reading too much into it all; he is just trying to unsettle me so I am not focused on the dispatch, which could make me navigate to the wrong setting. It is just not like him to help me.

Down the corridor, which is bright white, there are many doors, which are all also white – if not for the numbers or signs on each door, you would not even notice them. I do not know what goes on behind these doors, but some of them have signs, *Strictly No Entrance*, so, quite possibly I will never discover what happens there. I have on occasion wondered if there are more doors, the existence of which we do not know, simply because they have no signage.

I finally reach the end of the long corridor; it seems to go on forever. Things are a lot calmer here, and I encounter no signs of any urgency for dispatch.

Harry approaches and calmly greets me.

'Good morning, Rupert. Are you ready to start transition?'

'Yeah, Harry, but you don't seem to be in too much of a rush.'

'Ah, you know me, Rupert. I take things in my stride, but you will notice that I get everything done all the same. Now follow me to stage one.'

'No probs. Lead the way.'

I enter, and a warm glow hugs me tight. Everything here is usually so white and bright that it is a shock to my eyes to see another colour. I am to stay in stage one until my eyes adjust to a level safe enough to adapt to a less-bright environment. The furniture is also different; it is more 'earthy', made of wood and fabrics, rather than metal, glass and plastic that we have become adjusted to living here.

'Make yourself comfortable, Rupert. I will come back in a few minutes to bring you to the Vortex.'

'Thanks, Harry. See you then.'

I choose to sit in a big, sturdy armchair. I put my head back, and my phone rings.

'Hello?'

'Hi, Roo, what's going on? Are you okay?'

'I don't know, Syd. Maybe I am just paranoid after what we were all talking about last night, but Jayden met me in the dispatch entry in an awful panic to get me dispatched early. I am now in first stage and Harry isn't in any panic – but, you know Harry, he doesn't ever panic. What do you think?'

'You should just watch out. I don't think you can trust Jayden. I will keep an ear out, and if I catch wind of anything, I will send you a message.'

'Thanks, Syd. I appreciate you watching out for me, but all seems to be going smoothly here now. I had better go, because Harry will be back soon.'

'Alright, then, Roo. See ya.'

Harry knocks on the door and enters. He brings me over to check that my eyes have adjusted.

'Well, your eyes are ready, Rupert. If the rest of you is ready, we may as well get you dispatched.'

'Very cool sense of humour, Harry.'

'Maybe for you, Rupert … but when you have said it as many times as I have, it soon loses momentum.'

'Oh, right. I thought I was the first.'

'Sorry to disappoint you, Rupert … Well, you didn't answer me. Are you ready to go?'

'Oh, yeah. Sorry, Harry. I suppose so. Yes, I am ready.'

'Have you got everything with you? You know I can't stop once I have started.'

'I'm right to go, Harry.'

'Right then. Follow me, young man.'

We go through to the Vortex room, which is quite big. Right in the centre is the large oval-shaped Vortex. It is about ten feet tall and six feet wide, and it has a washing-machine effect in the centre, as it swishes around and around – faster than you can imagine. Its sheer intensity never ceases to amaze me. Every time I witness the magnificent phenomenon that is the Vortex, I feel part of something bigger than big.

'Please take your position and focus on your destination. When you are ready, give me the thumbs up.'

I take position, I focus, I give the thumbs up and I enter the Vortex.

'Alright then, Rupert. Good luck and goodbye.'

Chapter Three

Carrie

I can only describe the setting as picturesque. Green fields, farm animals grazing, the sun shining through the fluffy white clouds. In the distance I can see the outline of a castle. In front of me is a cottage, freshly painted white, with a bright-red front door. The cottage is very old, but someone must live here, as I can see smoke coming out of the chimney. It is quite like the old Irish cottage John Wayne and Maureen O'Hara emerged from in scenes of *The Quiet Man*.

Some activity catches my eye. A tall handsome fellow has just left the house; he walks down the adjoining field to what seems to be a building site. I must check this file to refresh my memory: yes, it says they have applied to move to another country, so why are they building a house? All this seems somewhat complicated, but maybe that is the reason for my coming – to bring some clarity to the situation and put their lives back into perspective if they have lost their way. I will not know for sure until I observe some more.

A young woman carrying a small boy comes out of the house.I recognise her as Carrie. She also carries her handbag, and she seems flustered. She approaches the tall handsome fellow. I must assume, at this point, that he is her partner. He doesn't seem happy; I can hear him grumbling away but can't make out the words.

'Okay,' she says, 'I am off to playgroup. Is there anything that you want me to bring back?'

'Just my son in one piece, please. Oh, and sometime today. Thanks.'

'Please don't be like that. I'm just going to playgroup …' She sighs. 'Would you like me to bring you back something to eat today?'

'Don't worry about me. I will be okay. I will just work away here, building a future for us while you go out socialising. Did you ever stop to think that I might need to go somewhere?'

'Well, do you?'

'That's not the point! What if I needed to get something for the house?'

'But you know that I go to playgroup every Wednesday.'

'How could I forget? You never know when to come back. I would die of starvation before you would think of coming home.'

'I'd better go. See you later … if you need anything, call me.' She walks to the car, with her head lowered and her heart broken.

Carrie's aura is one of intense sadness, yet no tears will come because she numbs herself to emotions so intense that they ripple through her, deflecting on those around her. I can only imagine how this type of home environment affects their young son. I do believe she takes the boy to playgroup in order to get away from this destructive atmosphere for a bit, even if only once a week.

Her partner comes across as harsh and hurtful, but he must have a reason for this spitefulness – maybe he is calling out for help and she is ignoring his cry because she is so caught up in her own struggle. She must fight to survive each day as she struggles to overcome the post-traumatic stress she still experiences. I wonder how they have come to this unhappy, torturous place in their relationship; suddenly, it all becomes clear why I am here. How can so much sadness exist in a place of such beauty? If only they would open their eyes and let the beauty that surrounds them enter into their lives, they would naturally feel more fulfilled.

Before I go any further, I must find out more. I open the box and look at the beautiful gems, taking out the one intended for Carrie. Her gem glows brightly as I look into its core to discover the secrets that lie in her and her partner's past. I see the cottage, with three people – two men and a woman – gathered in a cosy room warmed by a roaring fire.

They seem merry as they enjoy some alcohol. But as time progresses, the two men start to aggravate each other. One is so drunk he can barely stand up. An arm raises a bottle, and the drunken man falls to the floor. The other man continuously punches the fallen man in the head as he lies on the floor, unconscious. The attacker strengthens his blows by holding a little Buddha statue in his clenched fist. The woman is on the phone, frantically trying to get help. The man won't stop and the beating has gone too far. All the while she is on the phone, the woman is trying to stop him, a crying baby in her arms. In a panic, she hits the man on the back numerous times. He bolts towards her, enraged, and pushes her across the room. She remains upright, sailing to a corner of the room, with her baby cuddled in her arms, thankfully unharmed.

She shouts, 'Get out! Get out!'

The man runs out the door and drives away. The other man lies unconscious, bleeding from his ear; the woman kneels beside him, trying to wake him, but he does not respond. The intense shock hits her like a strong right hook: this might be the last time she sees her partner – the father of her child. So much time, love and energy invested into one person, and yet it could be all gone so quickly. The ambulance comes and the drivers enter the cottage to see a young woman sitting on the floor. She cradles a crying baby in one arm while her free hand strokes the face of her unconscious partner, whose head she nestles in her lap.

She keeps repeating, 'He tried to kill him, he tried to kill him ...'

The next few days take a toll. Her partner, discharged from hospital, lies in a dark room for days, trying to heal from the inflicted damage. At the same time, her own reaction kicks in, taking the form of post-traumatic shock. Her body shakes wildly if she talks about what happened, and a darkness has engulfed her thoughts. She realises that the attack has changed everything; she cannot fix things no matter how hard she tries. She blames herself for what happened because she invited the attacker – her own brother – into their home. She feels trapped between her love and loyalty to her partner and her love and loyalty to her family. Her family reacted to the incident by protecting her brother, justifying his actions in order to ensure that neither a conviction nor a revenge attack would result.

Yet, this incident is not the only reason Carrie now suffers from post-traumatic stress: it was merely the catalyst that pulled the trigger. Other elements have built up inside her, and these have grown out of control, attacking her soul far more than the attack itself ever could have done. She has had to give up her passion for learning about teaching drama and discovering herself, and this has left a void deep within her – even worse, she has felt that she has no-one to talk to about any of it. Also, she has breastfed her son ever since he was born, and this causes heightened emotions. Add to all this her partner's depression and constant put-downs, all of which have certainly impacted her, and as she does not deal with them, they have stored up inside her, grinding her down, eating away at her confidence and self-worth. Financial pressures have resulted from her not working, yet she is still servicing debt in an attempt not to stress her partner further, as he would just become more depressed. It has been a juggling act for her, and no-one can juggle forever. The attack was one more ball too many – and so all the balls came crashing down.

Carrie's aura, once so vibrant with yellows and oranges, is now unclear and hazy – yet it is changing, and this indicates she has started a spiritual journey of self-discovery. All people do not encounter such dramatic changes in their auras, but when they do happen, they turn people's lives upside down, as individuals can sink to levels of deep sadness, possibly even trauma. If only Carrie knew that at the other end of her journey of self-discovery she will find divine happiness – and that, no matter what happens, she will be so in tune with herself spiritually that she will be practically unbreakable.

I need to go back to another significant time in Carrie's past. Back to a time where I can see and judge if she and her partner are a couple that should be as one. The scene shifts to three years earlier.

The scenery is the same, but the cottage is not. It appears rather derelict; the inside looks as if birds have been nesting there for years, and the outside is wildly overgrown and worn. I see a *For Sale* sign. A black sports car pulls up and a glamorous blonde steps out; she wears a flattering shirt, trousers and high heels. Her long blonde locks are highly styled and well maintained, and they shine in the sun as they flow down her back. She smiles a bright, confident smile. It is Carrie, but I hardly recognise her. Her aura glows so intensely, it seems on fire; if only she knew the world is her oyster and she has decided on this place. Why? Out of the driver's seat hops a tall, handsome man. He, too, has a vibrant aura, but Carrie's is so intense, it outshines his.

'What do you think, Tom? Can you do anything with it?' she asks.

'Well, I'll have to take a look inside, but I thought it would be a lot worse.'

'I just love it! I think we can make some money on it if you can do it up a little to make it liveable. I will get the grant for it and then you can build …'

'All right, Carrie,' he says as he puts his arms around her waist. 'Let's just take it one step at a time and see if we win the bidding war.'

'Oh, so you mean that you think we should take a chance and do it?' she says excitedly. She looks deep into his eyes, leaving him no option but to say yes. He loves her with all his heart and he wants her to have anything she wants.

'Yes, if you're sure …'

'Oh, I'm sure, hon! Thank you!'

They passionately kiss, not unsettled at all by the curious neighbours who drive past.

'Can we at least look inside before I totally condemn myself, though?'

'Oh, yeah! Follow me – I think it has so much potential.'

They push open the makeshift front door and enter the cottage.

The scene shifts to six months later. They are both at the cottage again. I sense this place is a big part of their lives. The outside looks wonderful; Tom has cut away all the overgrown bramble and weeds, which are now in a pile of ashes in the adjoining field. He has painted the outside of the cottage a gleaming white, fixed the front door and painted it fire-engine red. Tom approaches the cottage while Carrie is inside, painting. The inside is liveable once again. Tom has built a strong fireplace with his own two hands, and the walls are brightly painted in whites and creams to give a sense of freshness and space. He comes into the house, puts his arms around her and kisses her tenderly on the neck.

'I have to show you what I have found!' he says excitedly.

'What is it? Tell me, please …'

'No, I have to show you. Follow me.'

They both go outside and walk around to the back of the cottage.

'Look, Carrie – it's a baby horseshoe! How lucky is that? It's a sign that we are going to be lucky here.'

'Oh, Tom! How cute is that? We have to keep it. Hold it upright, or all the luck will fall out.'

'We can put it alongside the big one that I found.'

'The little one can be for Baby,' she says, placing her hands onto her lower abdomen.

'It sure can, hon. I cannot wait to meet the little mite!' He places his hands on hers, and they look lovingly into each other's eyes. They kiss deeply, totally in tune with one another. Two hearts beating as one.

'Right. Let's get back to work, or we won't be moved in before Baby comes with all these distractions.'

They walk around to the front of the house, stopping in the front garden to look at the home they are creating. He wraps his arms around her.

Snuggling into his embrace, she says, 'This is our first family home, Tom. I don't care if the cottage is old; we have made it our own.'

'It sure is perfect, hon,' he agrees. 'If we want to get moved in, we had better get a move on!' He slaps her lightly on her bum.

She giggles like a schoolgirl with a crush, smiling as she walks back towards the cottage.

Their little gem has tired itself, so it loses its glow and stops there. It is a lot to take in, and I will have to take a timeout to absorb this introduction; the situation is more complex than I thought. This cottage also seems to be significant, so I will have to investigate it further. It is so unfortunate that Carrie and Tom have lost their way, as they were truly happily in love. Their hearts that once beat as one now miss each other's beats entirely. They need to stop walking different paths and come together again.

I shall move on to observe my next assignment. I must focus on the destination, so I shall take a walk down the lane to absorb some of the naturally beautiful scenery that helps cleanse the mind. I have found that nature acts like a filter. When we allow it in, it gets rid of the entire mass of unwanted gunk that clogs up the mind, thus assisting in making things seem so much clearer.

The stroll clears my mind, and I am now ready to move on.

Chapter Four

Tracy

I have not had to travel far. In fact, I do believe Carrie and Tracy have met frequently; however, their friendship has not yet blossomed. Tracy lives in a small town, so her environment is not as picturesque as Carrie's. I stand in front of Tracy's home, which is a terrace house facing a cul-de-sac of older terraced houses. The front room has a large window, and I imagine this allows her family to observe many goings-on, keeping them in touch with the outside world. The initial vibe from this house is significant, emanating much grief and sadness. This home has a lot of death connected to it, and this has taken its toll on the family.

Tracy has received many gems, but only one gift so far; yet she has desired so many. I do not know why they have been held back, but I do recall her profile outlining a medical problem. I enter the house and see an old woman sitting on a chair in the kitchen, having a cup of tea and a bun. The kitchen is small, with a big table that dominates the floor space. A matching pine dresser holds plates with a topiary tree design. The cupboards are fresh and clean. The walls are painted in neutral colours, with a central row of stencilled topiary trees all the way around. I have a feeling she likes a theme. A woman I recognise as Tracy is standing at the kitchen sink.

Through the bright white net curtains, she watches her young son playing with his dog. Observing her lovingly gaze outside, I know her only wish right now is to provide her son with a brother or sister.

Tracy's mother looks at her daughter, knowing what she is thinking.

'Don't worry, love,' she says. 'You will get another one someday.'

'Someday, Mam? I can't wait until someday. I'm almost forty, and Joey is getting older.'

'I know that, love. But stressing yourself out about it isn't going to do any good, is it?'

'But they said that at your age, Mam …'

'Women go through this all the time, love. You need to focus on what you have.'

'How can you say that when you know how much it all means to me?'

'But, love …'

'No, Mam! I have heard enough,' she says. 'Come on, Joey!' she calls through the open window. 'It's time to get ready for playgroup.'

'Yeah … coming, Mammy!' he calls back as he skips across the yard.

Tracy's sister enters the house, calling, 'Hello! Good morning, all!'

She walks into the kitchen with a fake smile on her face, and seeing her mother look sad, asks, 'What's wrong, Mam?'

'Nothing, love, it's just … oh, nevermind.'

So she calls from the kitchen to the adjoining living room, 'Tracy, what's wrong with Mam?'

'What's wrong with Mam?' shouts Tracy. 'Are you kidding me? You should ask what's wrong with me.'

'I'm lost here. Who is going to tell me what's going on?'

'Well, love …' their mother begins, but then Tracy storms back into the kitchen.

'Mam has told me that I need to get on with things – I should stop thinking about having another baby, and I should get over the miscarriages I've had because women have them all the time.'

'Mam's right, Tracy, it's all gone on for too long. If your mother can't tell you the truth, who can? You're not helping yourself or Joey by acting like this. It's starting to be impossible to be in your company. Is it any wonder Rob can't wait to get out of here for any opportunity he finds?'

'Well, that's a lovely thing to hear coming from your own sister!' Tracy snaps back. 'Come on, Joey. We're going.' She storms out with Joey in tow and slams the front door behind her.

Wow! Tensions run high in this house, too. With heightened tensions come strong emotions – and although it is hard to hear the truth because it hurts, it is necessary for us to face it so we can move on. Through conflict comes change. Tracy wears her heart on her sleeve: if she is feeling down, everyone around her will know, and those who are closest to her will possibly feel down, too.

Tracy's aura is red and pink, which means she is a person with no hidden agendas. She is not afraid to make her point of view heard, as people with a mostly red aura are usually quite direct. They readily move on from different hobbies, jobs and the like, as they can get bored easily. I see that, for Tracy, this has resulted in her not having an outside interest; her main focus is her family. The slight pinkness in her aura shows she is strong-willed and expects high standards from others. She has strong ideals and definite opinions about which morals and values are acceptable.

I do not know why this lady has been chosen to receive yet another gem. I believe it will tip her over the edge and cause some mental instability because she has experienced each of the gems she already has received as a trauma. The support of her family seems to be dwindling, so she is likely to suffer more intensely the grief of any further loss.

I take out the box of gems and see that Tracy's is glowing.

It needs to show me something, so I look into it intently.

It is the same house, but we are upstairs in what I guess is Tracy's mother's room as there are a lot of flowers and lace. There is a dressing table covered with a lace cloth, and on it are numerous objects: a jewellery box, talc, perfumes, prayers and other things accumulated and treasured over the years, each one with its own memory. Tracy wears a nightgown with a pussy cat on the front; it looks like a long light-green T-shirt. Her mother is lying on the floor and has obviously had a fall. Tracy helps her back into bed, making sure she is settled and comfortable. She reads her mam some verses from her favourite book of poems.

Kissing her on the head, Tracy says, 'Goodnight, Mam,' and gets up, switches off the bedside lamp and walks to the door.

She doubles over; the pain has made her drop to the floor, and she crawls out into the corridor, where she calls for her hubby. He comes running out, shocked at what he sees.

'I think it's the baby, Rob. Please help me. I don't want Mam to hear.'

Bending down, he picks her up in his arms and carries her to bed.

'Is there anything I can get you before I call the doctor?'

When she says no, he runs downstairs and calls the after-hours doctor, who promises to come round straight away.

'The doctor said to make you comfortable; he should be half an hour at most,' Rob tells Tracy. 'Here is a drink of water, love.'

'I don't want a drink of water! I want this pain to stop … I want our baby to be okay.'

Their son calls out from the other room; he appears to be about two years old. Rob goes to see to him.

'Why is Mammy crying, Daddy? Did she hurt her knee?'

'No, son. Mammy is just sad, but she will be okay. Sometimes it is good to cry if you are sad.'

'I don't want Mammy to be sad, Daddy.'

'I will make Mammy happy again, son. Don't you worry. You go back to sleep and have some cool superhero dreams.'

'Okay, Daddy. Do you promise?'

'I promise, son. Goodnight.'

'Good night, Daddy.'

Rob goes out into the corridor, hears a knock on the door and goes downstairs to answer it. He leads the doctor upstairs to the bedroom, where Tracy lies sobbing. Rob waits outside the door. After a few minutes, he hears her cry even more. He buries his face in his hands as if he is going to break down also, but he doesn't.

The doctor comes out into the corridor, closing the door behind him.

In a whisper, he tells Rob, 'She is going to need to take it easy, and she will need a scan in a couple of days. It looks as though she has lost her pregnancy, and so she will need a lot of support. I have given her something to help her sleep tonight, and I would like her to visit me tomorrow.'

'Yes, Doctor. Thanks for everything,' Rob says.

'I'm sorry I couldn't do more to help. I will let myself out, and I will see you tomorrow.'

'Okay. Goodnight, Doctor.'

Rob opens the bedroom door, only to see the love of his life in so much emotional pain that he feels helpless to ease. They look at each other, and he rushes to her side. He puts his arms around her, holding her in his warm embrace all night long as she continues to sob.

I move on to another time. The gem brings me to the same house, but it must be a few years earlier. The shifts in time are not as clear as they were with Carrie and Tom.

I see Tracy and Rob, somewhat younger; they giggle and laugh, snuggling on the sofa. They nibble from a box of chocolates while watching a movie.

'Everyone is going to wonder why we're not out tonight.'

'Don't worry, Tracy. We'll just tell them we're saving.'

'Yeah, I know, Rob. But we always go out on Friday night, so they are going to suspect that something is up.'

'It's only for a few more weeks, and then it will be all done. We will be Mr and Mrs.'

'I know. I can't wait! But our ones are not going to be impressed that they didn't get a big day out, you know.'

'Ah. Well, sure isn't that why we haven't tied the knot yet? No, we're right to do it our way, Tracy. You even said yourself that you wouldn't feel right walking up the aisle without your dad. God bless his soul.'

'I know you're right, and it is just for me and you, Rob. Just as it is we that have to live together for the rest of our lives – living as one, having lots of children … it's all so exciting! I never thought I would feel this way, or I would have done it a lot sooner. Why didn't you ask me sooner, by the way?'

'Sure, you have always put me off by saying the things that you say, and with all of the things that have happened. Anyway, don't think of that now. It is happening, and I couldn't be happier.' He passionately kisses her on the lips.

Her sister walks into the room, all dressed up ready to go to the local pub.

'Are you sure that you guys aren't going to come out for a few? Mam is all settled, so no worries there.'

'Nah, we're okay here. It'll do us good to have a few weeks out of the pub.'

'You mean you're not going out next weekend, either? It's Dave's birthday, you have to come.'

'Yeah, we'll see, sis. You guys have a great night.'

'We will. You guys have a good, boring movie night.'

'We will!' Tracy and Rob say together, looking deep into each other's eyes and giggling.

'You two are up to something. I just know it. It's not right to keep secrets in a family, you know.'

'Yeah, we know. See ya, sis.'

'See ya,' her sister says and reluctantly closes the living room door.

'Oh, I can't wait to see her face when we get back and tell her! She'll go crazy. Mind you, I don't like lying to Mam. Do you?'

'No, of course not, but look at what happened any time before. There has always been a death or misfortune, so I thought we were agreed that this is the best thing to do for everyone.'

'Yeah, of course, it is best for all, especially now that this baby is coming.'

The gem stops there. It seems as though this family has endured a lot over the years. I can see why Tracy has a heavy heart. She would truly benefit from having a chakra clearing, as this can help anyone who may constantly experience bad luck. But, forTracy, it would be especially beneficial, as chakra clearings help those who have difficulties moving on, or who are anxious, unhappy, confused or depressed.

To have come from such a place of love and joy – with both her and her potential hubby hoping to have a big family – to now, with all that joy and all those hopes dwindling, it is no wonder Tracy is so distraught. She has endured the pain of losing what she has worked so hard to get, and this has destroyed her emotionally.

Deep down, she may even hold her mam accountable for her first pregnancy loss, though she has never said anything – she just allows it to eat her up inside. Tracy would never inflict such guilt onto her mother, no matter how harsh her words might be at times. All this has led to Tracy being resentful; her focus cannot shift to anything else, and she cannot move on. Her urge to have a sibling for her son is so intense that it consumes every thought, which results in her slowly isolating herself from friends and loved ones. She needs guidance to enable her to get back on the route to happiness. And that is why I have been sent.

Chapter Five
Bethany

I arrive in a city and stand outside a tall apartment block. Drawn to go in, I arrive at apartment number eight and enter. It is spacious, with windows all the way around framing a wonderful view of the city. I have always perceived man-made creations as ugly, but when seen from this vantage point, I can only describe the view as breathtaking. Inside, the apartment reminds me of where I live: the white walls, the pristine white leather sofas, the glass tabletops and the metalwork – it all seems designed as if from Heaven, looking down onto the Earth. Whoever thought of this design is a creative individual. A large white bookcase with hundreds of books dominates a section of the apartment, standing out from the rest of the furnishings.

The apartment is the site of a lot of activity; people seem to be rushing around organising things. Someone has a hairbrush in one hand and a styling iron in the other. Another person scurries about, setting up cameras in different locations. Someone else dictates everything and he has everyone in a panic. Things need not be so chaotic.

I eventually locate a young woman whom I believe to be Bethany, but I can hardly see her because so many people are around her – styling her hair, putting on her make-up and dressing her, all at the same time. It all seems so unnecessary; if they each took a turn, it would be a lot easier. *Is this her home?* I wonder.

Everyone rushes around that little bit faster, and then, in an instant, they all stop. It looks as if they are playing musical statues and someone just turned off the music.

'Bethany, *da-a-arling,* would you like to follow me? We'll take our first picture here on your sofa. I'm thinking a relaxed, I-love-being-at-home look.' His French accent is fake or highly exaggerated.

She lies down on the sofa and holds a pose, asking, 'Likethis?'

'*Pe-e-e-erfect,* sweetie. Just hold it there.'

A last brush of powder dusts her already perfect face, and a last pump of hairspray mists her long chocolate brown locks. (I have always wondered why they do this; it is not as if one brush of powder and one mist of hairspray at the last second will make any difference.) Bethany doesn't move an inch; she is almost a statue.

'Well, is everyone ready? We want to get this shoot wrapped up in time, so we need to get into position. Bethany, darling, when do you think your handsome Hanson will get here?' enquires the same man. His French look comes complete with beret, moustache, neckerchief and tight trousers. In short, he is a sight to behold.

'Oh, I don't know, Claude. Did your people get in contact with him to confirm? He didn't mention it this morning.'

Worriedly, he calls, 'Justine, did we get a confirmation from Hanson's people for ten o'clock?'

She quickly answers, 'Yes, we did, Boss.'

'Well, can you call them again to find out what time he is expected?'

She gets on the mobile to locate Hanson's whereabouts. 'His guys have said hes hould be here, Boss. They'll call him and get back to us ASAP.'

'Thanks, Justine. Keep me updated.'

Her phone chimes again and she answers it before the second ring.

She turns around to see everyone looking straight at her, waiting expectantly to hear the outcome of the conversation.

'He's getting a sausage roll at the deli down the street; he will be here in five.'

Trying to hide his anger and frustration, Claude shouts, 'Okay, we will focus on our single shots first.'

At that moment, Hanson strolls into the apartment, eating a sausage roll. He has a confident, casual way about him that would frustrate some; he appears to just take life in his stride, never succumbing to the constant fast-paced demands that everyone else here seems to exhibit. He is like a breath of fresh air – he's not the most handsome chap in the world, but he definitely has a 'presence'.

When Bethany sees him, her love for him glows from within. This sends Claude into a spin and he calls for a five-minute break.

Bethany gets up from her pose, gliding across the floor with a little skip in her step. She stops at the spot where ten people hover around Hanson like bees around a hive. When he sees her coming, he shoos them away to make way for Bethany. He acts as if he hasn't seen her in a lifetime, yet he only left the apartment a few hours before.

'Beth, is everything okay?'

'Yes, hon. I'm all the better for seeing you.' Standing like a schoolgirl with a crush, she twists her feet and looks straight into his deep-blue eyes.

'Come here,' he says passionately, exuding confidence as he grabs her in a tight embrace. She practically disappears in his arms, she is so thin.

A few moments later, Claude starts a commotion, trying to get a photograph of this moment of tenderness.

This is so lovely to observe. I can see Bethany's gem start to glow, even in the wooden box, and I gaze into its core to discover more about her past. It brings me to a large family home, with the stately grandeur of an older style – a lot of rooms but few people to fill them. I see a man, a woman and a beautiful young girl. I believe this to be a young Bethany, possibly at age eleven. The man and woman, whom I take to be her mum and dad, seemto be having an argument while she looks on.

'No, Harry, she must go to the competition. If she doesn't win the state heat, she doesn't qualify for the national heat. She just must go! I am not letting her ruin her future just because she wants to go to her friend's twelfth birthday party.'

'You're exaggerating, Hil. There will always be lots more beauty competitions … sure, how many has she already won this year? It would be healthier for her to go to her friend's birthday, because that's what she wants to do…'

'It would be more beneficial to her future to go …'

'She needs to spend time with her friends.'

'She sees her friends every day in school.'

'Yes, school. How much of that has she missed because of comp—'

'I was wondering when you would bring that up.'

'She needs an education, Hil, she's not going to be so young and beautiful forever.'

'That's why she needs to make the most out of modelling now, so that she is set up for the future.'

'No, Hil! You just want her to succeed because you didn't.'

She slaps him hard across the cheek, her face red with anger.

'Just stop it, both of you!' shouts Bethany through her tears. She has been crying all along, and they didn't even notice – or maybe they just didn't care.

'I can't please both of you, so I am going to my room.' Bethany storms off to her room and no-one follows. They start bickering all over again, this time about who was responsible for upsetting her.

Bethany feels so alone and unloved. How sad it must have been for her to grow up in that type of environment. Parents always want the best for their children, but they tend to enforce their ideals rather than letting the child have room to discover their own ideals for themselves – thus discovering themselves naturally.

The gem moves on a bit further. It seems to be a few years later, and Bethany is about sixteen. They are still in the same house and her mother is getting her bag ready. As her father walks in the front door, her mother holds out her hand for him to give her the car keys.

'We are away, Harry. Your dinner is in the oven. Come on, Beth, or we'll be late. We don't want that Josie to get chatting to the judges before it starts.'

Her father doesn't even respond, he hands over the keys, drops his bag and takes off his coat.

Bethany kisses her dad on the cheek as she goes past him. 'Goodbye, Dad.'

He kisses her cheek, too. With a smile, he says, 'Goodbye, love. Good luck tonight.'

'Thanks, Dad.' She shuts the door behind her.

How sad that things have deteriorated so much between her parents. All has certainly had an effect on her attitude towards relationships. I sense that she blames herself for the years of bickering and also for the years of silence.

The gem pulls me to another time. The setting is a nightclub; it seems to be a more upper-class establishment from what I can make out.

One of the big men standing at the door approaches Bethany, saying, 'Follow me, Miss.'

He leads her and her friends past a long queue of cold girls in short skirts, high heels and low-cut tops. They look at her with jealous hatred as she passes.

Once inside, the big man escorts her to the VIP area. It seems that only a select few and their friends have access to this area, which has a private ba rand its own waitresses, so VIP guests need not battle any crowds at the bar. The dance floor, situated in the centre of the room, has its own well-renowned DJ.

Bethany has caught the eye of a young man across the room.

One of her friends says, 'Look, Beth! Hanson Jones has been checking you out since you walked through the door.'

'No, he hasn't,' she answers shyly as she sneaks a quick peek.

'Yes, he has, Beth! Wait until you see … he so has the hots for you.'

Hanson watches her for a while. When he catches her eye, he smiles and she smiles back. He stands up, straightens his clothes and shimmies across the empty floor to get her attention. He approaches her table, gets on his knees, and says, 'Where have you been all my life, beautiful princess? Can I have this dance?'

Knowing who he is, she blushes with embarrassment at the scene he has made and the attention he is giving her.

Everyone in the room has stopped to stare, waiting to hear her answer; it was as if he had asked her to marry him. In the distant background of her pulsating brain, she hears the music change to a slower pace.

She answers, 'Yes, I would love to. Thanks.'

The relief is clearly apparent on the young man's face, as I do not think he ever had to wait as long for an answer before. He stands up, swoops her into his arms and twirls her around. She giggles and he carries her to the dance floor, where he sets her on her feet as carefully as he would a porcelain doll.

They dance all night, holding each other close but without saying a word, so comfortable are they with each other. Their hearts are beating as one right at this moment, and I can see they never want to separate.

The gem's light dwindles at this point, and I have gained enough insight into Bethany's past. I stand and observe her aura: it is one of purples and some green, colours that further enhance her beauty. The purple has struck a chord, explaining the bookcase: people with purple auras are born to learn about a wide range of subjects, which tends to make them knowledgeable and interesting. This is not a colour I would expect a model to have, but those with predominantly purple auras can be perceived as mysterious and secretive, which further explains the colour. The presence of green suggests she prefers to have things thoroughly well thought out before acting upon them, indicating she is not impulsive and doesn't like surprises much. Oh, this could be a problem – but I won't jump to conclusions yet.

It is now time to move on.

Chapter Six
Kath

I arrive in a busy town with some definite hustle and bustle, but not the unfriendliness I encountered in the previous city environment. People are talking to one another other and waving as they drive past those they know. Life here has a slower pace, but seems to offer a more meaningful existence. So many people work hard, focusing on 'bettering themselves' in order to move on to somewhere else – usually a place that millions of others who already have 'bettered themselves' have moved to as well. Cities of 'better' people imagine this is so. However, I beg to differ. I believe people 'better themselves' from within, not by means of the qualifications they obtain and the jobs they secure.

I finally catch a glimpse of a woman I believe to be Kath. She has just parked her little red sports car in a reserved spot outside a fitness centre. She gets out of the car and walks fast towards the centre's doors. She has a presence about her and looks fit in her tight black yoga pants and crop top. I didn't expect her to live in such a small town because her profile states that she often appears on TV and has her own line of fitness DVDs.

I enter the studio, where she stands in front of a group of about sixty people (mostly women). Posters of Kath line the walls and she is talking the group through the steps of her newest DVD, giving them the opportunity to try some of the exercises with her before they commit to investing in her latest workout program. She explains that this new DVD complements any of her earlier DVDs they might have purchased.

'Hi, everyone! Thanks for coming today,' she says. 'Well, as you probably know, this is my hometown, and I always love it when I get a chance to come back here to catch up with everyone. Unfortunately, I don't get to stay long, as I just stop over on my promotional tours. This tour is for my newest DVD, which one of you lucky Energisers will win today simply by being here. So what are we waiting for? Let's get started!'

Exuding the motivational energy she began to create when she spoke to the audience, Kath walks over to a stereo bearing her logo, *Energiser,* and puts on some funky music to get a rhythm going.

'All right, Energisers, let's get those energy levels heightened. We'll start with a warm-up, and then we'll progress to a higher energy-boosting level; just stay at your own pace, where you feel comfortable.'

This goes on for ten minutes, and I have to admit she gets me energised, too – I even tried a few moves while observing from the sidelines. To be able to make others feel so good inside is a good thing, and Kath is a good person for doing this. I can understand why she has dedicated her life to helping others by introducing them to the world of exercise. Initially, I thought she was selfish for wanting to follow her career and accumulate wealth. But during this short time of observing her, I have changed my opinion. I now believe that for many years she has sacrificed her own desires to settle down and have children so she can keep energising others, because this is what she is good at and she genuinely wants to help people.

I view Kath's aura to give me a clearer picture of her. It is significantly blue, which is a rare dominant aura colour. Many world leaders, in fact, have blue auras, as individuals with a mainly blue aura are successful in engaging others. People with blue auras are born leaders who effectively communicate their beliefs, are well-organised and successfully motivate others. This draws me to look deeper, and I discover a shadow, which indicates that a secret from the past follows Kath. Her profile does not contain this information; she must have hidden this secret so deep within herself that she believes she has erased all traces of it from her mind. I must investigate this further.

Her gem starts to glow, right on cue. I gaze deep into the gem, observing that I am still in the same town, albeit some twenty-five years earlier. People are on the streets chatting with one another. Everyone seems to be going in the same direction, so I follow.

We all arrive at a big green field, which seems to be the site of a fair. Stalls are set up to attract adults and kids alike – with candy floss, hot food, small toys and such, all to make a quick profit on the one day of the year the town comes together in the same place.

The atmosphere is that of a feel-good community day for the whole family. All sorts of competitive games are on the agenda. The men line up to pull tug of war, which is a must to win, as bragging rights will belong to the winning teams and their supporters (wives and children) for a full year. The horn blows to start tug of war, and then the only sound heard is a mighty 'heave ho!' The men dig their feet into the muddy ground, pushing their legs as hard as they can in a desperate bid to secure a win for their team. I scan the field, observing other games, including the three-legged race, the egg-and-spoon race, and the greasy pole – always a favourite, as each person tries to get to the top of the pole in order to obtain the large amount of cash dangling from the top.

I spot a girl I think is Kath. If my calculations are correct, she is about fifteen. I'm surprised to see she is pleasingly plump, given how fit and slim she is now. Perhaps she has not yet outgrown her baby fat.

She and a handsome young lad are holding hands, giggling while they run around the big performance tent and hide behindit.

'I hope no-one has seen us coming around here, James,' she says.

The lad reassures her. 'Don't worry, Kath. I made sure no-one saw us.'

He goes to kiss her, but she pulls back. 'I thought you liked me, Kath.'

'I do, James. It's just …'

'Just what? Don't tell me that you're gonna get all fidgety on me.'

'No. No, James, I promise I won't.'

She lets him kiss her, and he puts his hand up her top. He always seems to push the boundaries with her. They do this for a few minutes, lying on the grass together, and then he sits up.

'Are you still up for me coming around to help you babysit your little cousin at your house tonight?' he asks.

'Yeah, of course … if you still want to, that is.'

'What time are your parents going out?'

'I heard them tell Uncle Harry that they would leave at seven, so come any time after that.'

'Are you still up for … you know?'

'Erm, eeh …' she stammers.

'Ah, you're just unbelievable, Kath! I might just not bother coming around at all. You obviously don't like me. We've been going out for a whole five weeks now,' he says in a slightly raised, highly irritated tone of voice.

'I'm sorry, James. It's okay … I'm just a bit nervous. You promise it won't hurt?'

He pulls her into his arms and hugs her. 'I wouldn't hurt you, Kath. You're my beauty queen.'

She smiles, feeling treasured in his warm embrace.

The gem moves on at this point. I have arrived at a two-storey country house with wonderful gardens. The fragrance of wild roses fills the air with a perfume one could never capture in a bottle, just cherish in memory. The house is at the edge of the town.

Inside the living room stand a man and a woman, both looking rather stressed. The woman is crying, and she sits down while the man begins to quickly pace the floor. Kath, wearing her school uniform, sits on a chair. She is crying, too.

'I'm sorry, Dad,' she says. 'I didn't mean for this to happen.'

'Sorry? Did you hear that she said "sorry"? The stupid girl doesn't know what she has done, does she?' Her mother doesn't answer.

'You have always been such a good girl, Kath. You pass all of your exams, you study well, and everyone likes you. You could be anything that you want, but you go and throw it all away. I just can't believe it.'

'I'm sorry, Dad.'

'Who is the father? Who did you let take away your innocence?'

'I can't tell you, Dad. You are too mad.'

'You're not going to tell me who it is that has ruined your life? Well, there is only one thing we can do.'

At this point, to Kath's obvious relief, her mother speaks up. 'We can't make any rash decisions, love. We must think this through.'

'There is nothing to think about, love. We are good Catholic people, so we can't get it terminated. She is just going to have to go to the nuns.'

'No, Jim. We can't send her away!'

'We have no choice, Sue. We cannot let anyone find out about this; our whole reputation that we have built up our whole lives will be destroyed in one instant. We will just tell everyone that she has gone to visit your sister.'

'Please, Mum, don't let him send me to the nuns! I'll stay in my room. I promise I won't go anywhere. Please don't let him send me away!'

'Do you think that I could live in the same house with you? Just watch as my daughter's tummy swells with a child that has no father? No way, Miss! You are just going to have to leave, and that's the end of it! Now go to your room; your mother and I need to speak in private.'

Kath goes to her room, where she cries all night and throughout the following day. It isn't long before the nuns from the local convent come to take her to a hideaway, where she will stay until she has her baby. The nuns will place the baby witha couple who cannot have children.

I am brought forward six months to a disturbing sight. A young woman is screaming and crying. She has just given birth to a baby girl and a nun is already taking the baby away.

'No! Don't take my baby! Give her back to me. I want to hold my baby.'

She tries to get up to run after the nun who has taken her baby, but another nun restrains her. This doesn't take much effort, as the girl is greatly fatigued after eighteen hard hours of labour.

One of the nuns says, 'Hush now, it is for the best. What kind of life would you be able to offer a wee one? Sure, she doesn't even have a dad.'

'I will loveher!' the girl shouts hysterically.

The nurse gives her an injection, saying softly, 'There now, you will feel better in a moment. Just relax.'

The girl cries, 'She's my baby!' She breaks down in tears, and then she slowly drifts off into a deep sleep.

I now see Kath in a totally different light. How traumatic her life was at this point and how alone she must have felt! And then to return to her parents' home to act 'happy family' again so people would think she was away at her aunty's for six months must have made it even worse.

I feel like I need to observe a positive, happy experience she has had. Thankfully, the gem starts to glow, giving me the opportunity to do just that.

I seem to still be in the same house, but Kath looks a few years older. The atmosphere feels happier. Her mother is calling for Kath excitedly; she has an envelope in her hand, and she is holding it up to the light in a desperate attempt to view the contents.

'Katherine, come quickly! You have a letter from McLloyds University. It must be about your application.'

Kath comes running down the stairs. She seems to have lost a lot of the teenage plumpness that she had a few years before. She has been working out upstairs, I gather, noting the towel around her neck and the sweat on her brow.

'Thanks, Mum,' she says as she takes the letter and turns to go back upstairs with it.

Her father steps out of the front room, saying, 'You can just bring that in here, young lady. We are a family. We all deserve to hear the outcome of your application.'

She gives him a look as she reluctantly enters the room. They have obviously not resolved their issues. I also sense the reason she does not want to enter this room is that this is where her father made the decision to send her away.

Kath tears open the letter, reading it to herself but saying nothing.

The suspense is too much for her mother, who finally asks, 'Well, what does it say? Did you get the place?'

'Yes, Mum, I have been offered a scholarship, as I had the highest marks of all the applicants.'

'Are you sure it is sports science that you want to study? You do know that with your grades you can study anything at all.'

'Yes, sports science, it is. I'm sure of it. Exercise is my life, and I am going to help others benefit from it, too.'

'It's a waste of a good brain, if you ask me.'

'Ah, Jim, leave her. She is happy now,' her mother says. 'And she is going to university, so you should be happy, too.'

'It's just such a pity, is all; she could have studied law or medicine or anything. That's all I'm saying.'

Turning to Kath, her mother says, 'Well, I am proud of you, love. You have achieved so much, and I hope it all works out for you.'

'Don't worry, Mum, it will work out for me. I'll make sure of that. I am finally getting my opportunity to get out of this town, and I am not going to mess it up.'

The gem stops there. It is all so much clearer now. I can see why Kath has invested so much of her life in exercise. With her aura, she was destined to be successful – and what a bonus to be successful at something she is passionate about! I understand why she wanted to move away from this place, as her father never forgave her for the teenage pregnancy. Although she has not expressed it, she will never forgive him for what she had to endure. By deciding to move on, Kath has made a sacrifice: by not taking any time out from her regime, she has not been able to meet anyone to start a family of her own. Maybe she doesn't want to, as she knows her daughter is out in the world somewhere, and Kath feels empty because she doesn't know her – doesn't even know who she is.

This visit can only help make Kath face up to her unresolved issues and make decisions for her future.

Chapter Seven

Siobhan

I am back in the city; it is a fast-paced street. People walk past each other as is they have turbo boosters attached to their ankles, leaving them incapable of stopping for a chat. Should any people stop, it would be at their own peril, as others would surely mow them down and trample them on the pavement. It is like a sea of heads, and the survival technique is to go with the flow – or pay the price. This sight of so many people doing the same thing, even though they are each totally individual in character, never ceases to amaze me.

A building draws me. I read its sign, which has large gold letters: *Maximus Corporation.* It is an old limestone building that stands out architecturally from the adjoining glass-panelled skyscrapers that dominate the skyline.

I stand outside for a moment to observe the woman I believe to be Siobhan among the crowd. Her appearance sets me back at first, and I try to remember what Boss said to me the night before dispatch.

I recall his words: 'Remember the profile, Rupert, because what is inside is not the same.'

Yes, of course. I know that it's what's inside that counts; I must catch a hold of myself.

Siobhan starts to head towards the door where I have positioned myself, and I repeat Boss's words in my mind: *Rememer the profile; what is inside is not the same.*

A man sits on thepavement in front of the door. He holds a cup that he shakes, looking for some spare cash. She ignores him totally.

'Any spare change, lady?' he asks.

'Go get a job and a life, you sponger. People like you make me sick,' she says, with venom in each word.

The man lowers his head and does not reply. Her words were harsh, and they kicked him right in the pit of his stomach when he was already feeling quite low. People like Siobhan should take more consideration for others' feelings; not everyone has a heart made of iron. What she said could be detrimental to the mental and emotional stability of this man.

Her immediate reaction towards him assists me in overcoming my initial setback, and I am able to focus again.

I continue to follow her into the building as she thunders her way through the lobby towards the lift. People in her path stop whatever they are doing to greet her.

'Good morning, Miss Roe!' they say. I hear it so many times that it reminds me of listening to a harmony.

She just storms past these people without even acknowledging them or their greetings. The guy at the lift door must be new because he appears nervous and looks towards the other staff for support.

They attempt to indicate what he should do by signing to him but apparently it is too late.

In the midst of it all, Siobhan starts to speak quite suddenly and the other staff put their hands over their faces.

'Young man, aren't you going to greet me? Why don't you have the lift waiting?' she demands. 'I want to see your supervisor straightaway. This is most inconvenient.'

The tongue-tied young man cannot even answer her.

'You must be new. I do not want this to happen in future. Ever. Do you understand?'

The young man nods excessively to indicate his compliance.

Finally, he is able to speak. 'Yes, Miss Roe, I understand. It won't happen again, Miss Roe.'

'I certainly hope not.'

She then enters the lift alone, even though a queue of people still wait in the lobby, all of them needing to get to work on various floors.

As the lift door closes, she says sarcastically, 'Where do they get these imbeciles from? Do they just pick them up off the street?'

She arrives at the top floor, bursting out of the lift as soon as the doors open. Once again, all the people stop what they are doing to greet Siobhan as he storms past. A young woman runs to assist her with her bag and coat, which Siobhan practically throws at the girl.

Siobhan's office is on the opposite side of the building from the lift. Her walk across the floor is more like a stampede designed to ensure everyone is aware of her presence. When she enters her office and closes the door behind her, everyone sighs in relief.

The young woman who took Siobhan's coat and bag follows her into her office. She hangs up her coat, sets down her bag and straightens out her desk.

Meanwhile, Siobhan continues to move about, never ceasing

her frenetic pace. She walks back and forth while looking out of the massive Georgian-style window.

'That boy at the lift downstairs, Bea. I want him fired,' Siobhan tells her assistant.

'But, Miss Roe, this is his first …' says Bea.

'I don't want to see him there tomorrow. Do you understand?'

'Yes, Miss Roe. Will that be all for now?'

'Where is my coffee?'

'It's coming right up, Miss Roe.'

Cautiously backing away from Siobhan, Bea opens the door and goes out, closing the door noiselessly behind her.

Siobhan is in a league of her own. I am not at all surprised to see that this woman's aura is a fiery red. People with dominating red auras usually have a lot of stamina and physical energy. They can be spontaneous, and their presence will be dominant, no matter where they are. They easily get bored with others, so they tend to isolate themselves; also, the effort of making friendships is a pointless exercise in their eyes. If something holds their interest, success and wealth can prevail. They also are straightforward people with nothing to hide. I have never witnessed an aura quite like this one. It is as though the fires of hell blaze around her. Red does not necessarily mean 'bad' – in truth, no aura is bad – but when a person like Siobhan uses an inner anger to fuel her character, while expressing it so freely as to fail to consider the feelings of other people, it is a recipe for causing them emotional pain.

Siobhan is a well-renowned lawyer, which does not surprise me. This suits her character, as the law appeals to her; each case is different, so her work holds her interest. Maybe she is bored now she has made her wayto the top of theladder. I believe she did enjoy climbing it, although I hate to imagine what terror she must have left in her wake.

Her gem starts to glow, and I look inside reluctantly because I expect that what I am about to witness will not be pleasant.

I am in the same building, but it is a few years earlier. It looks like Siobhan's office, but it seems to have belonged to someone else at this time – the decor is different, and a framed photograph of a woman and child sits on the desk.

A woman has her back to me. Her red hair cascades down her back in long waves. She and a man are in a compromising position on his chair. She sits straddled across his lap, flirting seductively. She stands up, lifting her leg in a way that makes her short skirt ride up her perfectly shaped thigh to reveal a suspender and lace-trimmed stocking.

She whispers, 'My panties are crotchless. Would you like to take a look?'

He sits there, as if in shock, and then he nods. He appears to be a lot older than her.

She sits up on his desk, tucking her foot under his chair and pulling it towards her. She places each foot on an arm of his chair, giving him a full view of her crotch.

Bubbles of sweat start to form on his head and he mumbles, 'Oh, gee … it's beautiful.'

To which she replies, 'Would you like to kiss it?' He nods again, so she pulls his head forward.

She tells him what to do as he sticks his head under her short skirt, and then she takes a quick peek at the clock when he can't see. I find this extremely odd.

Lifting his head from under her skirt, he rises off the chair. 'I know this might be unprofessional of me to ask, especially as I am your mentor, but do you think that we could … you know …?'

'Mr Baker, what are you implying?' she replies in an innocent tone.

He backs down onto the chair and says, 'Oh, I'm sorry! I didn't mean to …'

She takes another quick look at the clock and moves around the desk.

Suddenly, she lies back on the desk, opens her legs wide and says, 'Please just take me, Mr Baker! You don't know how long I have waited for this moment.'

Wasting no time, he jumps up from his chair, all empowered, and confidently pulls her to the edge of the desk. He enters her, thrusting with all his might.

Just as he is about to climax, the door bursts open and a woman stands in the doorway. It is the woman in the photo. Horrified, she stands frozen to the spot for a moment before she screams.

Quickly composing himself, he runs over to her. 'How could you? How could you?' she shouts.

'I'm sorry, love. I really am.' He begs her to forgive him.

'I got a call to meet you here so that we could go for dinner. Did you want me to find out this way? Do you love this …' Looking Siobhan up and down, the woman finishes with, 'this girl?'

'No, it only just happened this once. Someone has set me up, love.'

Siobhan gets up and walks past them, brazenly saying, 'Excuseme,' so that they have to move out of her way as she leaves the room, closing the door behind her.

The gem moves on a bit in time. Siobhan is now fully dressed in a respectable suit, a total contrast to the seductive attire she wore the night she seduced poor Mr Baker. She is in a conference room, the only woman among a small group of men in suits gathered around a large table.

One of the men stands up, saying, 'Thank you all for being here.

As everyone knows, over the past few months Mr Baker has been suffering a nervous breakdown and will not be able to return to his position in this firm for some time. As the board, it is our job to appoint a new member to our team. I think we all have come to an agreement, Siobhan, that we would like to have you join Maximus Corporation as one of our top lawyers.'

Siobhan acts all shocked at this announcement.

He continues, 'The work you have completed during your time with Mr Baker has shown that you are a very capable lawyer, and so we would be honoured if you would accept the position we have just offered. Obviously, this is a big decision, and you may need to take some time to consider it …'

'No, no, not at all. I would love nothing more than to become a member of the team here at Maximus Corporation, and I would like to thank you all for thinking of me. I know I could never fill Mr Baker's shoes, but I promise I will endeavour to do my best at all times.'

The man who has been speaking is the head lawyer; one of the other men calls him Bill.

Bill says, 'Welcome to Maximus Corporation, Siobhan.'

Everyone stands up and claps, and then, one at a time, they all turn to shake her hand.

Has this woman no shame? First she ruins the man's life, and then she takes his job.

I need to look back into her childhood to see where all this vindictiveness stems from. I hope to find some answers there.

I look deep into the gem, and it brings me to a place that is already familiar. I realise it is the same town Kath is from. It is a small world, indeed. A pub on the main street draws me: Roe's Bar. At the door stands a tall man smoking a cigarette. People are beeping their horns and waving in their cars as they pass by.

A person shouts, 'Hey, Roe, see ya tonight!'

He waves and answers, 'For sure, Mac, see ya then!'

I enter the bar; the fusty smell – a mixture of alcohol and cigarette smoke that is enough to make anyone barf – assails me. Behind the bar is a woman with red hair like Siobhan's, but this is many years earlier so it can't be her. Perhaps it's her mum. The woman has her back to me, so I can't see her face. She seems to be arranging glasses. I go closer to the bar, and now I can see a little girl helping the woman. The child also has red hair, so I guessed right: this is her mum and this is Siobhan as a child; she appears to be about six.

She says, 'Mum, where will I put this one?'

'Let me see, darling. Oh, better not touch that one, pet. That is Daddy's special glass.'

The little girl starts to panic, and she accidentally drops the glass as she passes it to her mother. It smashes into pieces on the floor.

I am taken back by this woman; her aura and her appearance are so strikingly like …

Forcing myself not to get lost in my own memories, I focus on the scene.

The man at the door runs towards the bar, enraged.

'What was that? Can you two do nothing without making a commotion?'

'It was just a glass, dear. Nothing to worry about,' the woman tells him, winking at her little girl.

'At the rate you two are going, we'll have no glasses left! We are in business to make money and you're not helping by smashing our profits on the floor around you.'

'Calm down, Mike. It's not good for Siobhan to see you so cross.'

'Cross? I have good reason to be cross. What is she doing in here, anyway? Come on, out you come! Get back upstairs. Do some reading, colouring or some such thing.'

'But, Daddy, I'm bored.'

'You are a child. Go and find yourself something to do. Just get out. We're trying to build a future for you here.'

Head lowered, the little girl walks slowly out from behind the bar, where her mother is on her knees with a dustpan and brush, frantically trying to erase any evidence of what was actually smashed. She looks relieved as she empties it all into the bin.

'Wait a minute. Get back here, Siobhan!' her father says suddenly.

Siobhan freezes on the spot, and so does her mum. Each has a look of horror on her face.

'Where is my glass trophy that I won for "Publican of the Year"?'

They don't answer, for fear seems to have taken control of their bodies.

'I mean it, Rosie. Where is it?'

She gulps. 'It was just an accident, Mike …'

'I knew it! Everyone upstairs right now! Can I have nothing? Get over here, you stupid girl. What happened? I need to get to the bottom of this.'

Her mum quickly runs to lift Siobhan and carries her upstairs. Once there, she continues to hold Siobhan, cradling her in her arms to protect her.

'Put her down, Rosie! You can't protect her from the world; you know she has to face up to what she has done. Do you know how much that trophy means to me? You know I worked hard to get it.'

'Of course we know, Mike. We helped you, remember?'

'For all you did. Now tell me what happened.'

'Well, we were … It wasn't her fault.'

He grabs Siobhan by the arm and drags her out of the room.

She is crying, her small body heaving in convulsions of fear. 'You are going to spend the rest of the day in your room until you learn not to touch things!' he roars. 'I knew that I was never supposed have had girls. Give me a cub any day. You will never make anything of yourself, stupid girl.'

'Leave her alone, Mike, she's done nothing wrong, I dropped the glass.'

Dropping Siobhan on the floor, he storms back towards his wife.

'Well, you can just fix it, you clumsy bitch.'

Grabbing her by the arm, he drags her downstairs to where she deposited the glass fragments into a bin liner.

'Mummy, I need you!' cries Siobhan as she creeps back downstairs.

'It's fine, love. Mummy will get you in a moment. Just go up to your room and I will be with you soon.'

'No, you don't! You get over here and see what happens to people who tell lies and then try to cover it up.'

He makes her mum take the shattered glass out of the bin bag, piece by piece, with the sharp pieces cutting her hands. It is painful, but she does not let on because she does not want to upset Siobhan even further. The little girl is already horrified at witnessing the way her father has humiliated her mother. The woman sits all day with a tube of glue, sticking the glass back together piece by piece.

When she finishes, Siobhan's father comes over to her. 'Look at the set of that!' he says as he grabs the glass and smashes it into the bin.

'Now go sort yourself out, woman. We will be opening up soon.'

The psychological trauma endured by this child throughout the years has obviously left its scars. She has decided not to be the walkover her mother was. Siobhan loved her mother very much and knew she did all in her power to protect her from her father's rages. She always wondered why her mother never left him but believes it was because she felt she couldn't. Fearful of losing her daughter, she endured all the agony for Siobhan's sake. Her father suppressed her mother so much that she became brainwashed into believing she was worthless and had nothing to offer her child. If only she had been confident enoughto realise her daughter only needed love and protection from her. Because of this childhood environment, the adult Siobhan decided to be the controller, not the controlled.

It always fascinates me to see how the victims of physical or emotional abuse usually go on to become abusers themselves. I reckon it is a defence mechanism. If only they would decide to break the cycle of abuse, they would discover they are far more powerful and in control by showing love and respect for others than by being abusive. Abusers choose not to control their behaviour, thereby knowingly inflicting pain on others – especially the people they love – and when this happens, they are not in control and often do things they later regret. Nevertheless, none of this takes away the abuse.

I see Siobhan in a new light, and I now understand the roots of her vindictiveness; however, I do not condone it. I understand why she has been chosen for a visit. Her head is so far up in her own personal cloud that she needs to be brought back to Earth to deal with the emotions she suppresses.

Chapter Eight

Rupert

Of all of the initial observations I have carried out to date, the last one has affected me the most. I have realised that I, too, have issues I have not dealt with. I knew Siobhan was going to resemble my dearly beloved late wife, which did shock me when I first saw the photo in the file, but it wasn't until I witnessed Siobhan's mother's presence that my heart skipped a beat. Her tenderness and devotion to her daughter brought back a flood of treasured memories; I was not fully prepared to experience this. Her mother's aura was so warm, yet bright and angelic, like my Josie's. Tears gather in my eyes, and I feel I must take time out to gather myself, as this has knocked me off track, big time.

It all brings me back to a beautiful time we shared together. It is many years ago. Josie and I are on our honeymoon. Nowhere fancy, just the seaside a few towns away from our hometown, but that doesn't matter – we don't intend to do much sightseeing. We want a big family – boys and girls –it doesn't matter as long as they are healthy. I know exactly the moment we receive our gem.

We are in our little cheap beach house that we've rented for two full weeks – after looking forward to the trip for months – and we have not left the house for days. It has reached the stage where we may starve to death if we do not get out of bed soon. I can just imagine the headlines: *Honeymooners Die of Exhaustion and Starvation!*

Have you ever been so happy at one moment in time that you never want it to end? Well, that's how Josie and I feel. We are so afraid of not achieving the same level of oneness again after we move that we just stay wrapped in each other's embrace for days. Eventually, though, we have to give in and get up, lest we make headlines. That night, as we unite again, it is even more special than before. We have made love many times, but this time stands out, as we are completely in sync. Each thrust feels like Heaven; we groan together, and eventually and reluctantly, we come together – we don't want it to ever end. At that moment of total oneness, the lights flicker. We both feel the same shivers all over our bodies, and every one of our hairs stands on end in heightened sensation. It is the most magical experience I have ever felt.

Three weeks later we discover we are expecting.

'It happened that night, Roo, I just know it. It was so magical … it had to be when it happened.'

'I can't believe how perfect everything is, Josie. I need to pinch myself to check that I'm not dreaming.'

'Roo, it's destiny. We are as one, and we will never be apart.'

'I would die happy at this moment knowing that I have achieved the maximum point of tranquility,' I tell her.

I lift her up in my arms and swing her around. And then I carry her across the threshold of our two-bedroom cottage, which we fell in love with and were lucky enough to buy. It has roses in the garden that leave a lingering perfume all year long. (Whenever I smell roses, it brings me right back to that time.)

I will always treasure this moment. So much so that I have it tattooed on my brain for everyone to see, as I am proud to have been lucky enough to have intimately shared my life with the woman I will treasure forever. I will never feel that love again, and because of this, I know it wouldn't be fair to get involved with anyone else.

It's hard to explain how the effects of the emotional shattering we experienced a few weeks later turned it all upside down. The roller-coaster of life caught up with us. A few weeks earlier, we were on the highest point of the ride of life, and then we crash straight to the bottom. Quite simply, for us, the ride just stops.

We discover Josie has cancer in her womb; abnormal cells appeared in a smear test that she'd had just before we got married. It's like being shot in the stomach. All we see are doctors and more doctors. They all advise us to terminate the pregnancy, as this is the only way Josie will have any chance of survival. Of course, I knowshe will never agree to do that, as she is very in tune with herself and her spirituality. I remember the conversation we had about it.

'No way, Roo. I cannot kill our baby. Our child has come to us for a reason, during the most magical moment in our lives, and I will never destroy that.'

'But then you will not survive the cancer, Josie. You heard what the doctors said.'

'Of course I heard them, Roo. But God has sent us this test for a reason, and we have got to trust Him.'

'Josie, I can't live without you. If we just do nothing, you and the baby will die. I can't live with that.'

'We don't know that for sure, Roo.'

She sits upright in her hospital bed, puts her arms around me and kisses me so tenderly that my heart melts. I know in that moment that I must do as she wishes. As hard as it would be for me to terminate our pregnancy, Josie could never live with knowing she got rid of what would probably be our only chance to have a child of our own. I know this.

As the next few months progress, Josie's health deteriorates rapidly. It all seems so unfair – we were so happy, and in an instant it was taken from us. As she grows weaker physically, I grow weaker mentally and emotionally; but no matter how much physical pain she must endure, she never wavers in her spiritual beliefs. She prays a lot during this time – not for herself, but for our baby growing inside her, and also for me, so that I will have the strength to carry on. This I know because I often lie in the armchair at night, letting her think I am asleep so I can listen to her words of strength. I often wonder, *How can this woman be so selfless?* She is the one who suffers intense pain, yet she prays only for others. This shows me firsthand her essence, and I understand the wise saying: 'Our outer glow comes directly from our inner essence.'

My life now consists of going home to sleep, getting up, going to the hospital, and then going home again. This consumes my life; all I live for is to go and watch the life drain out of my wife's body. The once-rosy cheeks that flushed with shyness at times are now pale; her long, shiny auburn hair that flowed gently down over her shoulders is now dry and lifeless, tied back to reveal cheekbones in a gaunt face that once was soft and beautiful. The one thing that has not changed is her eyes – they are every bit as green, and the love and warmth they have always held and projected onto me every time we are together still shines forth.

Each day she gets a little weaker, yet each day she is thankful for still having the strength to hold onto her life – as the longer she can do this, the better chance our baby has of surviving. Her faith becomes stronger, while my resentment at having to endure such intense sadness also grows stronger. Why can I not have it all? My beautiful, healthy wife carrying our beautiful, healthy children – I would give anything to have this. A lot of men take this for granted, yet I would give anything to be in their shoes instead of mine.

I, too, try to pray: 'Dear Lord, please don't take my wife from me. We are as one; if you take her, you may as well take me, for my life has ended also. Please don't leave me on this Earth to suffer a life without her, as it will be no life worth living at all.'

But no matter how hard I pray, she never seems to get better. Each day she seems to get a little worse. *At least she is still here with me,* I often think. She does not allow the nurses to give her the full recommended dose of pain relief, as she believes it will affect our baby growing inside her. Each day, too, the baby grows stronger, slowly draining a little more life from Josie's already weak body. Yet Josie often looks down and smiles at our little bump. She does not say much, as the pain will not allow her to, but when she smiles down on our child, she doesn't have to talk – I know exactly what she is thinking at these moments, which is that it is all worth it if she can give our child life.

She is such a strong woman, so in touch with herself and her spirituality that she is also strong in her mind. Even though she is pale because of her illness, she still has a glow around her. (Later I will learn that this was her aura.) It is a white glow, visible to one and all. People with white auras are angelic, highly spiritually evolved and close to God.

Suddenly, I hear Josie's voice; she has not been able to speak for a week. 'Roo, you know I love you, don't you?'

'Of course I do, Josie, and you know how much I love you, too.'

'Even as much as you loved me that special night at the beach house?'

'Yes, of course, Josie. I would give anything for us to be back there right now. Those are moments that I will treasure forever.'

'Let's pretend that we are there, Roo. Will you hold me?'

I sit up on the bed beside her and hold her in my arms. I start to tell her about the sounds of the waves rushing up the sand towards us as we lie together, listening. I tell her about the birds that swoop constantly into the sea to catch some food for lunch. I describe the smell of the ocean; it's so pure and refreshing that it revitalises our bodies with every deep breath we take. I tell her how close we are in our unity; we are as one, two hearts beating together, never to be apart. She turns to me and smiles. She puts her hand on mine, and with all the strength she can muster, she drags it towards our little bump. I feel it move and kick, so full of life; I understand in that moment that she feels alive through this child. We lie together in the peace and tranquility of the moment, and then, suddenly, she leaves me.

Monitors start beeping, and doctors and nurses quickly surround the bed, rushing me out the door in their desperate bid to resuscitate my wife who lies lifeless. This goes on frantically for a few minutes, and it does not appear to be successful because I hear someone shout, 'Notify theatre that we are on our way. We have to get this baby out now!'

It is all a blur to me; I have known this would happen someday, but I had not prepared myself for the emotions it would involve. As a survival technique, my body simply freezes and I have an out-of-body experience. I watch as a glow leaves Josie's body, realising at that moment that God has called her to leave this world. I understand that because she is so special, He wants her to be with Him – I was just so lucky to have had the wonderful time with her that I did.

When I come back to my body, one of the nurses is saying, 'Rupert, would you like to come this way?'

I follow, as attendants push the trolley with my wife's resuscitated body to theatre to enable her to release our child into the world. I wait and wait to hear a cry, but it never comes.

At last, the doctor comes out of the theatre and says, 'I'm sorry, Rupert, but there were some complications …'

At this point, I run; I don't want to hear what he is going to say. I run out of the hospital and into the street. I run an drun, not knowing where I am going, just wanting to be with my wife and child, who have both disappeared from my life in an instant. I come to a high bridge and I jump. As I fall, I hear screams at first and then, nothing.

I cannot go on without them, the pain is too much to bear.

Right after I jump, I begin my search for Josie and our child.

I don't reach the gates of Heaven, as I am not worthy because of the suicide. Instead, I am introduced to the Boss. He explains the rules: I was not granted access to Heaven because I took my own life, but I am a good soul inside, and so I have the opportunity to complete my journey to divine spirituality, which will allow me to enter Heaven – and I know my wife and child will wait for me there …

That is why I do what I do, this is why I am on this journey. I have received the opportunity to earn eternal happiness through helping others start on, or progress along, their own spiritual journeys of self-discovery, which will enable them to evolve to a spiritual level so they are closer to God and divine happiness.

I have come to see the contrasting differences in my life during those vital six months defined my existence on this planet, and for that moment, it was all too much for me to endure. It was a mixture of my fragile state of mind and the opportunity that presented itself to end the pain right there and then. One could call it circumstance or fate; I haven't yet decided which it was.

When I reflect now on what I did then, I know I was not thinking rationally. If I had been, I would never have thought of taking my own life. If I had stayed on Earth and endured the pain of my losses, would I have travelled on a voyage of self-discovery naturally? I don't know, and I suppose I never will know. I also will never know if I would have been more spiritually evolved when my life was naturally ready to end. Would I have gained instant access to eternal happiness? I don't know the answers to any of these questions, and again, I suppose I never will know. But, hey, at least I have this opportunity, and I am grabbing it with both hands. I did the wrong thing; I played God by taking my own life. I am lucky to know the journey I am taking is now focused on the right track, straight back into the loving arms of my Josie and our child.

Chapter Nine
Home Influences

Now I have had some time to evaluate my initial observations of each assignment, I can find a few connections and comparisons between them. What has drawn my attention, in particular, is the influence of the home environment – either the home where each now lives or the home from which each has come. Each woman seems to have a connection with an old house, and with every old house comes history.

Many people don't realise that when they buy or move into a house that has been previously occupied, they are bringing their energies and the spirits that follow them into that home, which already holds the energies of past occupants. Depending on the history of each individual house, this may never be a problem; however, I find on most occasions that it is necessary to spiritually cleanse the inside and outside of the new home to avoid upsetting any previously established karma which may cause problems when introduced to changes. The people in the home may never know what is happening in the darkness, but the negative energies projected will directly affect them, as this is unavoidable.

I will go back and study the energies of each significant residence in each of the cases.

I first arrive at Carrie's old cottage home. Outside, the aura of the home is quite aggressively red; this is not good at all, as the home should be full of natural colours which blend in with the natural environment in order for it to remain tranquil in its surroundings. Carrie and Tom are away.

I enter the cottage, only to discover the same aggressively red tone inside. The negative energies meet me at the door, almost pushing me away. Whatever inhabits this home does not want company.

'Who is here?' I ask.

There is no answer, which confirms my suspicion that the energies are not welcoming. A fiery-red glow is all I see. For this couple, it is like living in the belly of a beast; as long as they reside here while not spiritually cleansing the house, they are going to attract an abundance of negative things, because this house is negative to the core. They will never have any good luck living here. They must move on as soon as possible, or conduct an intense cleansing, which may or may not work in this instance.

It does, however, assist me in obtaining a clearer picture of how things have gone so wrong for this couple ever since they moved there. I remember what I first observed and then what the gem revealed to me: early on, they were so in tune with each other, their two hearts beating the same one beat. Now they are completely the opposite, where he will say anything to hurt her, and she is numb to feelings and expression – all because the two years they have lived here have taken a toll on them and the run of bad luck has continued without end.

If only they could see it themselves; listen to their subconscious minds or simply know when enough is enough, instead of enduring the suffering. They need to take control of the situation themselves and move on – or maybe that is exactly what they have done, and it is why they hope to move to the other side of the world. It is a waiting game for them now. A lot will change for them when they move. The energy in their house doesn't like them, but why?

I move on to Tracy. She lives in a terrace townhouse facing a cul-de-sac of older townhouses. Upon looking at the energies projected from the house, I notice that of all twelve houses in that terrace block, Tracy's stands out because of the dull gloomy colour it gives off. It even intrudes itself on the neighbouring properties, therefore affecting the positive flow of energy that should otherwise flow. With this type of energy colour, people often discover illness on their doorstep. Sadness and loss will also be quite prominent in the history of such homes.

I enter the house; this I do in a different way than when I am completing an observation of a person. I scan the home inside and detect the same energies I saw exuding the dull colour from outside. These energies bolt around the house, hitting walls, doors, ceilings and windows. If a window is open and one of the bolts escapes, the target it hits will have misfortune. For example, if a bolt hits a car, it may break down; if it hits a person, they may become ill. I can only imagine what effect this has had, and continues to have, on this family, each and every day. The family, however, will be more immune to the energies' detrimental effects. These energies will also affect visitors to the house.

'Hello! Is anyone there?' Icall.

'Yes, me,' says a dreary voice.

I follow the sound of the voice and see the spirit of a man sitting on the bottom step. His expression is forlorn, and he holds his face in his hands.

'Why have you not moved on?' I enquire.

'Do you really want to know?'

'Yes, please tell me. Do you know why I am here?'

'No, not really, but I am sure you have been sent to deliver something bad; I have seen it all over the years.'

'I have come to give Tracy an opportunity to change things.'

'Well, we'll see,' he replies.

'You were going to tell me why you are still here,' I remind him.

'When we first moved here, we were so excited to have secured a home for ourselves. But once we moved in we had nothing but bad luck. I got sick and died, leaving my wife to take care of four wee ones all on her own.'

'Are there any other spirits here?'

'Not that I have ever met, but when I first became a spirit, I saw that there was a reddish haze inside the house that I had never seen before – that is, I had not seen it when I was alive. It has now turned quite grey and dull.'

'Do you not feel that grey is better than red?'

'Oh, yes! That's why I am still here, you see, to make sure that my family is okay.'

'The red haze was a composite of leftover energies from previous tenants. When you and your family moved in, these energies clashed with the peaceful harmony of your energies. As you were the main protector of the family, you must have absorbed all of that energy flow, which resulted in your early departure from life. There is no more of that energy present now, only the dull grey energy that you project, but this causes sadness and misfortune for your family, although not as aggressively as the red did.'

'I didn't realise that at all. But my wife won't be here for long, so I may as well wait for her.'

'The waiting room at the gates of Heaven will present itself to you; if you move on, you can wait for your wife there.'

'I didn't know that,' he says, brightening. 'That sounds fine; see you, then.'

In a flash, he disappears, taking with him the dull grey energy that he unknowingly released and with which he infected so many. It has already begun to look brighter around here, and I catch a glimpse of yellow energy glowing inside. The people in this house will notice a dramatic change in their luck, for the better. This is an example of the instant, dramatic effects that result from having your home spiritually cleansed. I would go through a cleansing if I had it to do over again, but not a lot of people know about these types of cleansings, even though they surely must feel the negative energies draining them and making them ill.

I feel myself subconsciously called back to Carrie's house. The energies projected are the same, but when I enter the cottage, they are toned down slightly. A spirit of an old man reveals itselfto me.

'I'm sorry about before, but you can't imagine what I have had to witness here since they all moved in! You know, they're not even married and they are living together; "living in sin" is what we called that in my day.'

'Is that why you decided not to move on?'

'I have lived here all my life – and my entire afterlife up to now – and very happily, I might add. That is, until these intruding sinners came along and destroyed everything. Do you think that it is easy for me to watch this? Well, let me tell you, it's not. This is my family home; I grew up here, and then when I got married,

I raised my family here. It all seems so dirty since they moved in. This is my home.'

'But to cause them such deep traumas and sadness; do they deserve that?'

'I have to get them out! You don't understand.'

'If I promise that things will change to be more in line with your standards, will you agree to tone down your aggressive energies and consider moving on?'

'I will never move on, as I belong here for eternity, but I may consider easing my anger.'

'Well, that's all I can ask, then. I must go now.'

I leave him to it, for he is a prime example of a spirit that refuses to move on. Such spirits devote themselves to a property, and guarding it means more to them than moving on to eternity. I have tried to encourage him to move on, but he refuses, so this cottage will need a strong spiritual cleansing, which can only be conducted by a messenger of God.

However, I am pleased with the groundbreaking progress I have made here, and now I must move on to Bethany's apartment. It may look new and be filled with the most contemporary accessories, but the building is drenched in history. It is always harder to see a true energy ray when dealing with a multi-occupant building, as each apartment or flat will have its own history. It is worth remembering that your neighbour's energy can have a positive or negative knock-on effect on your own residence.

Bethany's apartment is on a corner block, and she is on the top floor, so at least she does not have to worry about the energies from above or to the right of her apartment. However, seven apartments are below hers, and as the energies always rise upward, her apartment may be at risk of being invaded by other negative energies.

From outside, I look up towards the sky, using my peripheral vision to absorb the energies projected from apartment number eight. The energy ray is like a rainbow; I see so many colours, some more significant than others. This is a concern, so I must enter her apartment in order to see what is going to greet me.

I arrive at the door, surprised to find that all seems calm. I enter, but inside it is no different: all is tranquil, with no sign of the chaotic, multicoloured aura I witnessed outside. Maybe I am losing my powers of reading energies; I must get my peripheral vision checked again.

On further inspection, I notice that lavender seems to be used as the number-one fragrance in the home. This is a relaxing scent which can also be used in the process of keeping a home spiritually cleansed. I see crystals hanging in different areas of the apartment, and these deflect negative energies.

I decide to check out the broom cupboard, just to be sure. When I open it, I see that what I suspected is true. There is a sea-salt floor wash present, along with a traditional broom. This is used to mark the floor area as the domain of the practitioner. The broom is used to sweep all the spiritual dust and dirt from the home by brushing from the back of the home to the front door. Bethany is obviously in the know about how to keep her home spiritually cleansed, as it is a miracle it has not been overrun with negative energies from the evidence I witnessed from outside. I have no concerns about a negative living environment with her. I have to admit, though, that I am curious as to why she is so conscious of this process. Have negative energies affected her before? I feel that I need to visit her past residence, as indicators lead me to suspect a concern.

With this in mind, I now decide to use Bethany's gem to check out the energies that surrounded her as a child. Her childhood home draws me once again. I believe that I have discovered the link between these five women. I am beginning to understand that the energies each one of them has been exposed to, or still is exposed to, within these residences in the past or the present, has had, or is having, an impact on the energies that have surrounded them up to this point in their lives.

As I approach Bethany's family home, the energies surrounding the grand house look familiar. As I recall, they are the same colours that surrounded Bethany's apartment block in the city. All the colours of the rainbow beam from the walls, indicating a confusion of energies. A cocktail of colours has built up over the hundreds of years that this stately home has been standing. As each new family took residence, the new energies joined the uncleansed energies that were there before. It is a cycle that would be great if all energies projected were positive, but it seems to be the negative ones that like to hang about the longest, and they have the biggest knock-on effect for the new inhabitants.

As I enter, I see a woman in a maid's uniform polishing a long wooden banister; I smell a woody, fresh scent that I remember distinctly from my past. I look into her cleaning bucket, but I do not see lavender or sea-salt wash, and she doesn't use a broom, so I conclude that she is not doing a spiritual cleansing.

The energies in this house are confusing. I believe different energies flow in each of the rooms, and I hear a lot voices echoing through the corridors, although nobody is visible. I feel that numerous spirits call this place home, but they don't want to make themselves known to me, as they must sense I am a messenger of some sort. I see their energies everywhere; by using my peripheral vision, I can see many glowing and gravitating orbs, which float freely all around.

I go toBethany's room, which is in the middle of the house, indicating that all of it affects her. As I watch her sitting on her bed reading a book, I realise that she has sat upright quite quickly. She appears to have sensed my presence. Her head moves as though she is scanning from one end of the room to the other. I am shocked to realise that she is using her peripheral vision to see me. I quickly depart.

Bethany is very connected spiritually both to her own being and that of everything in her environment, so the energies around her will have had more of an impact on her than the average person, as she can see them herself. I never cease to be amazed by this young lady; not only is she intelligent and knowledgeable, she is also so in tune with herself and so aware of the spiritual energies surrounding her. She must have been so scared here when she was a child, as, with her senses, she would have heard and seen all that I have, and on a constant basis. I can only imagine how it would have been for her, especially at night. (I have always believed that everything seems so much worse in the night-time.) Her mother's main focus was on enhancing her daughter's modelling career, her father worked most of the time, and she never had any siblings – she would probably not have shared her fears with anyone. Such a lonely, isolated childhood she had. I decide to move on now, as I feel I have witnessed enough.

Kath's childhood residence now draws me. I know it was an old two-storey homestead on the edge of a small town, so I am sure some unresolved energies still reside there.

As I evaluate it from outside, I do not initially perceive anything of concern. The house has character and charm, standing tall among the still taller trees that surround it. These trees obviously protect the home and provide its source of oxygen. I decide to enter anyway, because once I start an energy evaluation, I like to follow through so all of the boxes are ticked.

The first thing to happen catches me totally off guard, and I leap about ten feet in the air. A big fat hairy cat makes a leap for me, meowing wildly while it sails through the air. It could be mistaken for a young tiger, with its stripy fur and aggressive nature, but it is well-known that cats are sensitive to spiritual presences; in fact, they are the natural alternative to spiritual cleansings.

I am about to leave when I hear a timid voice call, 'Hello, dearie, can I help you?'

I turn around to see a little old grey-haired woman sitting in a rocking chair in a corner. The cat now sits beside her, purring as she gently strokes it.

'Oh, hello! My name is Rupert. I am a Visitor, and I was just hoping to check the energies in this house.'

'Oh, I see. Why would that be, dear?'

'I am hoping to help Kath find direction in her life, and I wanted to check out her childhood energy influences to see if they have a link to some issues she has had.'

'Well, I am Kath's gran, and I look after her just fine, dearie.'

'I am glad to hear that, Mrs …'

'Mrs Young. And, as you can see, Felix here helps me out in keeping the bad energies away.'

'I see that, yes, and what a great job he does, too. I am sorry to have intruded.'

'Nice to see a friendly face, dear. Are you sure that you won't stay for a cup of tea?'

'Thank you for the offer, Mrs Young, but I will be on my way.'

So, Kath has also had an influence with the spirits when she was young, albeit a positive guardian spirit. I can't see too much getting past her gran and Felix. Kath had a traumatic experience, though, when her father forced her to go to the convent, and her gran wouldn't have been able to protect her there. Given its history, I would expect to encounter numerous conflicting energies there.

I discover I am at the building where Siobhan works. This must mean that she doesn't spend much time, if any, at home. As it is an old and public building, I do not expect to see any specific colours to determine the energy influences that are being potentially absorbed. I channel in my auric sight and discover that the building has two significant colours projecting from it; each colour projects from different sides of the building, as if it were divided in two. One half is yellow, which is bright and fun, confident and positive; the other half is a reddish-orange, which signifies that the focus there is channelled on success and the desire to have the power to control others. Somehow, I do believe that this is Siobhan's side of the building.

I go in and up to the top floor, where I enter the room I believe is her office. Yep, it's her office, for sure – the energy flow is strong, whooshing past me as I open the door, flowing out into the corridor like a river that has burst its banks to affect the day of everyone it encounters. This room has been residence to many a power-hungry control freak throughout its history. Siobhan works long hours, spending most of her time in this room when she is not in court, and so it all has relevance, as it affects her aura.

I also want to quickly evaluate the energies that she grew up with in the pub. I have my suspicions as to what they were, but I want to check before it is time for release, and that is coming quickly, indeed.

Standing outside the pub, I can see the energies are really negative – greys, browns and some reds. A pub is often thought of as a hub for fun and communication, but in this instance, it is a cauldron of depression and negativity that can be detrimental to those residing and visiting. Add alcohol to the mix and it can be a recipe for disaster. I believe there have been many such disasters here. This would be a dark place for a child to grow up in; I would compare it to living in a deep, dark dungeon.

It is obvious the meanness within Siobhan stems from here. The controlling and power-seeking negative thoughts – which are the only kind of thoughts she knows – will only attract other negative things into her life. She leaves a trail of destruction behind her because she lives her life as if she were a tornado, destroying everything in her path.

It has been interesting to discover how the current and past energies have influenced each of their characters. I have witnessed enough to allow the gems to be released.

Chapter Ten
Releasing the Gems

If only they knew how close each of their gems has been to the other and how much they have discovered. This is the part of my job that I love; this is a magical moment that I never get tired of viewing – it's like the way you can watch a really great movie a hundred times and never get sick of it. Well, that's my opinion; not everyone will feel the same.

Back to the gems. I never know which one will release first, as I do not have the insight into when any of the women will undertake the dutiful deed, but the gems will enlighten me when it is time.

SIOBHAN

I immediately see one of the gems glowing, so I know it is time. I check to see whose gem it is and discover Siobhan is ready to receive. I am back at her office – my goodness, does she do everything here? I have not yet experienced her home, but I suppose these high-flyers think of their workplace as home.

I can see her. She has let her hair down and has a few extra buttons opened on her shirt to reveal her bosom. A dashing young man in his early twenties is with her. He is tall, with a lean frame, black hair and blue eyes. They are very close indeed. She has a seductive look in her eye, and he is a keen and willing participant.

'Check the door, Will; we don't want to get nearly caught again.'

He runs to lock the door while she clears her desk with one swoop of her arm. (This desk has been a prop for a lot of action over the years, it seems.) Rushing back, he pulls her into an embrace and holds her tight.

'Oh, Siobhan, you're so hot! Can't I just take you now?'

'No, you cheeky devil! You will have to earn your reward. I wouldn't be much of a mentor if I were to let you away with doing no groundwork, now would I?'

He buries his head in-between her breasts then uses his teeth to open the few buttons on her shirt that remain closed.

She pushes him away. 'Do your act, Will. Entertain me.'

He quickly obliges, backing off into the middle of the room and humming a tune that resembles a striptease song. He sways to and fro, smiling at her.

From her compromising position on the desk, she giggles; it is good to see her laugh. And then she shouts, 'Get them off!'

'My pleasure, madam,' he answers, quickly shedding his suit with disregard on the floor. Moving closer, he stands in front of her, wearing nothing but his bright smile.

'Come on, you eejit – take me!'

He quickly positions himself, and I get ready.

I hold out the gem in the palm of my hand; it glows with such intensity. The lights start to flicker with the power of the energy the gem contains. It lifts up off my palm and hovers in midair. In the next instant it zooms across the room with a light so brilliant it hurts my eyes. The gem meets its target as it enters Siobhan's body with a jolt. She sits upright.

'What the hell was that?' she asks.

'I didn't do anything wrong!' he says.

'Well, just don't do that again, Will. It wasn't funny.' She has obviously felt the intensity. The gem is now at work.

BETHANY

On we move as another gem starts to glow. It is Bethany's, and I find myself at a little cafe on her street. She is sitting with Hanson and they are gazing deeply into each other's eyes.

'Beth, you know I love you, right?'

'I love you, too, Hanson …'

'No, please, let me finish … We're always under a lot of pressure with the media and all sorts of things, and it's hard living our lives in the spotlight … But, darling, I don't think I would ever be able to live my life without you, and I was wondering if …'

'What, Hanson? Please say it.'

'Would you come to Paris next week with me while I film *Born Leader?*'

Bethany seems a little disappointed, and I'm sure she expected him to ask something that would require a little more commitment than hopping on a plane to Paris.

'Yes, of course I'll go to Paris with you, Hanson. It's also hard for me to be away from you.'

'How fantastic, Beth! You fill me with so much joy … I do love that top that you are wearing this morning. Is it new?' He beams a smile and winks at her. 'I have to admit it would look better on our bedroom floor … What do you say? When do you have to be at the studio?'

'Not for an hour … but I thought you had to …'

He grabs her by the hand and she hurries to her feet. They walk from the cafe to their building, still holding hands, and he eagerly pulls her up the stairs to their apartment. They are both eager as though this is their first embrace.

It doesn't take long for the gem to lift off my palm and enter her body. They are so close he also feels the intensity.

Holding her tight, he says, 'Oh, Beth! Did I hurt you? Are you okay?'

'No, you didn't hurt me. I just felt something strange, like a fuzzy glowing feeling entering me. It's hard to explain.'

'I felt it, too,' he says. 'I still feel a bit strange. Maybe we should lie here for a while to recover … we're obviously not ready to move yet, darling.'

And it is as if their fast-paced world has just stopped rushing around them. Without a care in the world, they lie together in each other's arms. His love and passion for her fill him, and this warms her heart and soul. She feels so lucky to have met him because she knows he loves her for who she is inside, not just what she looks like on the cover of a magazine – in fact, if he had his way, she wouldn't need to model, as he would far prefer to take care of her. This gem is in a good place.

TRACY

The next gem also takes no time in glowing, and I am happy to see it is Tracy's. I arrive at a hotel. Tracy and Rob sit at a table, about to have a meal.

'Five years married. Can you believe it has gone in so fast?'

'I know, Tracy. We surely have had our ups and downs since then.'

'Yeah, but do you remember the shock of it all when we told our ones what we had done?'

'It was priceless, but at least we have the intimate memories of our wedding that we always wanted.'

'You're right, Rob. Now, why don't we focus on tonight and making a few more memories for us to chat about next year?'

'I'm up for that! Do you want another vodka and tonic?'

'Ah, go on, then –it's only once a year.'

They indulge in a few more drinks and have their dinner. 'Why don't we just go home, love? I'd rather be at home snuggled on the couch with you than stay here much longer. I don't want you to be too drunk for memory making.'

'Yeah, come on, Tracy. Let's get the bill and go.'

On their way out, they bump into some old friends who persuade them to stay for one more drink, which of course leads to another, and so on. An hour and a half later, Tracy stands up a bit unsteadily and convinces Rob to follow her, as she promises to buy him a portion of curry and a battered sausage in the cafe. He follows her out the door, and they hold each other up as they walk down the street, singing quite loudly and out of tune.

Some of the people who live on the street peer out of their windows, shouting, 'Would you two keep your mouths shut? There are some decent people trying to get some sleep!'

They both giggle, and, with a white-paper parcel of fish and chips to share instead of curry and battered sausages, they quietly make their way home, knowing they will be the talk of mass if they upset many more people.

They arrive home and can't seem to get the key into the door; it is like a comedy act, as they are under the impression the keyhole is moving, not their hands. Eventually, they make it inside, finish the fish and chips and go upstairs to bed. (Gee, this has been the longest wait I have ever had to release a gem, and I may be missing an opportunity to release others, given the length of time these two have taken.)

Finally, they are in bed and the deed is done and over in a few short minutes. They do not experience the intensity to the same extent as the others, probably because they are numb as a result of their intoxicated state. In the morning, they may not even remember the event took place – but they will know soon enough.

The gem is in place and ready to help bring more hope to their lives.

KATH

Kath's gem is the next to start glowing. The setting where I arrive is strange, to say the least – not at all what I was expecting, but there you have a prime example of how expectations are sometimes presumptuous and can be shattered in an instant.

We seem to be in a ballroom; a disco ball in the centre of the room reflects sparkles of light all around. About fifty people, all of whom seem to be in their late thirties or early forties, stand around talking to one another. Most hold glasses of punch. I overhear a conversation.

'Oh, Frank, how you've changed! And to think I gave you up to date James, but thankfully, that was before he did the dirty deed with you-know-who. Did you hear she is a celebrity fitness instructor? Apparently she replied to the reunion committee and said she will be attending. I think it's terrible that she never had kids. She must be …'

'Can I stop you there, Francine? I think I see Carol calling me. Nice to see that you haven't changed one bit in all of these years. Take care now.'

'Oh, okay. Righto. I might see you again later,' she says as she slurps a big mouthful of punch which catches her breath and she starts spluttering.

Frank smiles a big fake smile. Under his breath he says, 'Not if I can help it, you won't.'

A big scuffle of people make their way towards the door, and I quickly realise they are approaching Kath; even Francine is making her way there.

Kath stands out from the crowd. She has a special glow that simply outshines everyone else's. This is what we mean when we say someone 'lights up the room'.

Kath makes sure she chats and is friendly with everyone, leaving each of them feeling fulfilled, connected to her, and a tease in her company. She spots James at the bar; he is on his own and looks in her direction, giving her a cautious smile. She stands listening to Francine waffle on about how much she loves Kath's new exercise DVD.

'I lost six pounds in just one week! You know, Kath, I wouldn't have believed it possible for it to happen so easily, as you know I have four children now … Oh, I hope that I didn't make you uncomfortable talking about kids … But as I said, I just told my friend Margaret about how good the DVD is, and she's going to buy it, too … So I am conjuring up some sales for you; maybe it would be a good idea if I did an ad for you …'

'Maybe we could chat about this again, Francine; it's been great chatting after all these years, but I must just go over …' Kath quickly makes her exit before Francine realises what she is doing.

Kath makes her way over to where James is leaning up against the bar and drinking a pint. He remains unaware she has appeared beside him until she suddenly asks, 'Would you like a drink?'

'Gee, Kath, don't do that! You made me jump just then ...'

'Sorry, James. Well, how have you been?'

'Ah, you know, same old: got married, got divorced, usual malarkey these days. You've been doing well for yourself, from what I hear.'

'Yeah, not bad. Life has been good to me since ...'

'Oh, so you left me here to pay the price, then!' he replies sarcastically.

'Don't be like that, James. You know it would never have worked between us – especially after all that happened – my dad just wouldn't have allowed it. I couldn't let him know it was you; he would have killed you, you know that.'

'Yeah, I guess, but it hasn't been easy, I can tell you. Now did you ask if I wanted a drink?'

'Is it the same again?'

'Why not?'

'Excuse me, barman, can I have a pint of lager, a vodka tonic and two shots of tequila?'

'For old times' sake?' James asks, curious.

'For old times' sake,' Kath replies, and they both knock back their shots, trying to catch their breath afterwards.

They happily chat for the rest of the evening, relaxed in each other's company.

'You know, I wasn't going to come here this evening, Kath.'

'No, neither was I, James. But I was curious as to how things turned out for you.'

'Yeah, well, I was kind of hoping you would be here, too. It's nice to see that we still get on so well. I don't know if you feel the sparks trying to ignite, but I do … or maybe it's just the tequila!'

'Oh, James, you crack me up sometimes …' she replies merrily.

He grins.

'Listen, James, I've had enough of this place and of my every move being watched. Do you fancy walking me back to my hotel? If you like, you could come in for a drink … I have a minibar,' she adds meaningfully.

'Love to. I'll just get our coats, shall I?'

'That would be great … You go on; I'll catch up with you.'

As she walks past Francine, Kath overhears her say to one of the other women, 'Well, she hasn't wasted any time getting reacquainted, has she?'

At this point, Kath has had enough, and she approaches the woman. 'Francine, about your offer to appear in one of my TV commercials. I must let you know that until you add another twenty pounds to the six pounds you say you've already lost … well, I couldn't even consider it, as we have levels of fitness standards to maintain … I do hope you enjoy the rest of the evening as much as I'm going to enjoy the rest of mine.' She walks away confidently, satisfied she didn't do what she had always done before, which was to walk away, say nothing and let others talk about her.

Francine is left with her mouth wide open, unable to speak. 'I bet that's the first time she has been speechless since birth,' says another of the guests.

As Kath and James arrive at the hotel, things progress quickly. Obviously a lot of passion still exists between these two; it has been suppressed for so long and is about to be released in one big expression. It starts in the lift. It is just the two of them, and as they look at each other, they cannot contain it any longer. The school-kid emotions come flooding out and they passionately kiss, leaning up against the wall. (What is it about lifts that arouse people? It must be the confinement.) They quickly have to straighten themselves up when there is a ping and the doors shoot open. An elderly gentleman gets in, looking at them strangely as though he has sensed the atmosphere.

They finally reach the door of Kath's room and she struggles with the key in the lock.

'Give it 'ere,' James says, taking control of the situation before he explodes with anticipation.

He gets the door open and they rush in, take off their clothes and embrace immediately. I get the gem out just in time for its release. They feel its intensity straightaway and its magical bonding powers keep them in each other's arms all night; holding each other tight, they just do not want it to end. I, too, remember that feeling.

Their lives are now going to change.

CARRIE

I am surprised that my last gem to release is Carrie's. I expected hers to be one of the first, as she lives with her partner. I expected they would have 'regular practice', so to speak. Nevertheless, as I have not been summoned yet I will have to investigate.

The little cottage is in darkness, and on entering, I discover the sleeping arrangements are not as they should be. She is sleeping on a makeshift bed in the living room with their son, and her partner lies alone in a big bed, unable to sleep – probably wondering how it all came to this, I'll bet.

Their relationship has deteriorated more than I had anticipated, so I must intervene. I have a small crystal, which, when released, ensures those in receipt fall in love for a time. This happens by means of the crystal's energy, which instils only positive thoughts and memories in the recipients; this should ensure they end up in a loving embrace. I would not usually take this action, but this is an extreme circumstance. This couple needs some special assistance because so much negativity and depression surrounds them. I sense that if only the negative energy would vanish – or be eliminated – Carrie and Tom would be happy with each other again.

I release the crystal, leaving it to work its wonders …

The next day I am delighted to see the final gem – Carrie's – has started to glow.

I begin anew. The scent of fresh flowers meets me at the door of the cottage when I arrive. Carrie and Tom are sitting in the living room. The atmosphere is calm and loving. A fire blazes, enhancing the warm mood. They are having a drink; she has a bottle of rosé and he has some cans of lager. The television is switched off for a change and they are talking – laughing and joking together, as natural as can be, talking about things they used to get up to and the risks they took.

'Do you remember the time we went to that Shania Twain concert?'

'Yeah, you wore those leather pants and all the girls were looking at you.'

'We never did make it to the concert, did we? We were having so much fun in that pub! I cannot for the life of me remember the name of it, can you?'

'We did get to the concert, Carrie. Sure, didn't I buy a Pink T-shirt?'

'Are you sure, Tom? A Pink T-shirt at a Shania Twain concert?'

'Sure, I'm sure; I wore it to the Pink concert that we went to after that.'

'Oh, yeah, that's right, you did. I don't remember much about the whole day, but I do remember leaving with all the crowds.'

'Yeah, and then we couldn't find the car, and with us supposed to sleep in it that night …'

'We went around in circles, and you were so peed off because I was so slow and giggling because I thought it was funny.'

'You were so slow because the heel had come off your boot, and you were trying to walk like you had an invisible heel.'

'I loved those boots, too, but they made such a noise when I walked because I needed new caps.'

'You don't have to tell me! Everyone could hear you coming a mile off. I was glad when the heel finally came off.'

'You should have said something if I embarrassed you.'

'Would it have made a difference if I had?'

'Nah, you're right … probably not. Do you remember that there were a lot of people sleeping in their cars in that field that night?'

'Sure, weren't we invited to join in a game of football at half two in the morning?'

'Yeah, those were the days, weren't they …?'

'Mmm.'

They both seem to be thinking back, and then, in no time, they are in a passionate embrace on the floor in front of the warm glow of the blazing open fire.

I prepare the gem for release. I hold out my hand; the gem glows brightly, lifts off my hand and zooms like lightning towards them.

'Wow! That was like dynamite, Tom.'

'You're too kind. Did I ever tell you just how beautiful you are?'

'Not recently, no.'

'Well, I'm sorry, hon. I won't leave it as long the next time.'

She smiles.

He kisses her tenderly and says, 'Now let's have another drink and do it again.'

As I leave, they are in each other's arms, reminiscing. I know I made the right decision to intervene, as I could tell they still 'had it', they just needed help finding it again. I believe they have made the first step to recovery; it will all turn out beautifully for them.

I have now released all the gems and feel quite lonely without them, as they have been with me for a while, assisting me with my observations. Now I must go it alone.

I wonder now, as I often have in the past: do the women feel it? Do they feel connected to something – to some power – in some way? Do they feel that something special has taken place? It always seems they do, but I wonder if I am sensing it because I know what will happen. Perhaps this will always be a mystery …

Chapter Eleven
Discovery

My messaging connector starts to vibrate, which is very strange as I usually am the first to initiate contact. I check the connector to read the message: *Roo, problem with gems – do not release! Syd.*

This has never happened before; the problem must be severe, indeed! I message back immediately: *Syd, release complete; what is problem? Roo.*

I cannot even imagine what has happened – maybe one or some of the gems were not ready, or maybe some change of plan as to who would receive the gems occurred. I could speculate all day, but that would be to no purpose. It would be just like me to run around in circles trying to catch my tail. I force myself to wait for Syd's reply.

Finally, I receive it: *One gem was gift. Jayden swap. C U soon at Vortex.*

I am shocked. I knew something was amiss at dispatch – Jayden was being unusually helpful and seemed stressed for no apparent reason, but to go to the extent of messing with the gems so I would get into trouble and lose my job because of negligence … that is too much. He has stooped to a lower level than I ever imagined he would. Syd was right to warn me to be cautious about him; it must have been her women's intuition. I should never have dismissed her concerns so quickly. Oh boy … this is a potential disaster! This could have quite a negative effect on the recipients as well as their gift because it was neither given nor received as intended.

I let Syd know I am on my way: *C U soon.*

I immediately make my way to the Vortex and she arrives at the same time. We both go through the Vortex.

'Roo, am I glad to see you!' Syd says. 'You wouldn't believe what has been going on since you dispatched.'

'It all sounds as though it has been somewhat crazy.'

'You could say that.'

'Come on, Syd, fill me in! There are so many things swimming around in my head and I don't know what could possibly have happened.'

'Well, remember I told you to be careful about Jayden …'

'Yes, yes – don't rub it in!'

'Well, I have to say, "I told you so". Sorry, Roo, but I had to get that out of the way first.'

'Syd, please …'

'Oh, okay. Well, when you messaged me from dispatch, I smelled a rat; it just didn't seem right, so I contacted Jonnie to see what he thought. He thought the same way I did, so we put on our detective hats and started to investigate. It was a bit impossible at the beginning, as Jayden never seems to leave his spot! Finally, Mother Nature called, and he went for a toilet break, which gave Jonnie and me time to check the gems and gifts. We found one extra gem glowing, as if in desperation at being left behind, so we knew to expect that one of the gifts was missing …'

'The son of a bitch! He has stooped to the lowest level of all! These poor innocent gems and gifts are too precious for him to use as weapons in his game.'

Syd continues, 'Right, Roo, the consequences are too high. Heads will roll when Boss finds out, he'll go crazy. So Jonnie and I decided to check the dispatch records. Sure enough, there was your signature on a dispatch release form for four gems and one gift to be released. You can imagine what a story Jayden had concocted to cover his ass.'

'This is going to end in disaster, Syd – I can just feel it. If only I had known this before I released them.'

'I know, it would all be so much easier, but there is nothing we can do about that now. We had better focus on limiting the damage.'

'You're right. Thanks for going to such lengths to help me. This could ruin any chances I have of making it into Heaven, and then I would never see Josie again … I couldn't deal with that.'

'I know, Roo,' Syd says softly. 'And that Jayden is just thinking of his own selfish desires, not even considering the consequences his actions could have on others. So many people can and will be affected by this one problem!'

'Well, there is not much we can do until we discover whose gem doesn't return.'

'I know. That is why I brought us some Heavenly delights to keep us going in the meantime.'

'Syd, you are so perfect! You know, if ever I was in need of a Heavenly delight, it is now, for sure.'

We sit on the top of a high hill covered in the greenest grass.

In silence, we devour two delights each while we look through the Vortex, watching the world flash quickly past us.

'You know, Syd, you never told me the story about how you ended up in the Waiting Zone.'

'You never asked. It's not something you want to think about every day, is it?'

'No, not really, I suppose … But I do want to know. Please tell me why you have to wait to enter Heaven.'

'It's simple and straightforward, really. I was living my life happily, working as a support worker for a mental health organisation. It was a job I loved – challenging but also very rewarding. I was working towards a future with my fiancé, Simon. We hoped to get married and have children as soon as possible.'

'That doesn't make sense, Syd. Why would you be kept from Heaven? You sound as though you gave so much to others and led a good, respectable life.'

'Yeah, I know, Roo, but you asked, so hear me out. Anyway, I'd reached a point in my life where I was so happy and was planning my future as best I could. That day … the day it happened … I had got up feeling particularly happy and told Si how much I loved him. We had been very close that morning, and Si wanted to have a duvet day because he had an unexpected day off. It was freezing cold outside, and I no more wanted to get out of that bed than he did. After pushing it for as long as I could, I eventually bolted out of the bed.

'I told Si, "Sorry, hon, I gotta go in … I can't let them down, they will be short-staffed and it will kill me all day to think that." He said, "Ah, Syd, it wouldn't kill you to just take one day off … right then, I'll make you a deal … meet me for lunch at Mauritio's?"

'"It's a deal," I promised. I kissed him and left.

'Are you sure you really want to hear this, Roo?'

'I've wanted to ask you ever since we met. I thought you didn't want to share your story. Unlike me – I wear my heart on my sleeve, and everyone knows what my story is.'

'Right then. Well, when I was leaving work at lunchtime to meet Si, one of the members jumped up out of his seat, gave me a hug and told me to take care. It sent shivers down my spine, but I promised I'd be careful and so he finally let me go.'

'That was a strange thing for him to do.'

'I know, but he must have sensed something. Anyway, I left and started on my five-minute walk to the cafe strip. I stopped at a pedestrian crossing; the wee man was red, so I waited. I could see the cafe, and Si was waiting outside in the alfresco area. He saw me, too, and waved. Just at that moment, an elderly gentleman came charging past me and straight onto the road.

'My immediate reaction was to stop him, so I stepped onto the road to pull him back. I pulled him to safety, and then all I could hear was a loud horn and Si screaming my name. As I turned to see what was wrong, the big lorry hit me. I still remember the initial contact.

'The pain, the shock, the realisation – they all rolled into one in that instant. After that, the rest was a surreal experience; I started to rise into the sky, leaving my barely recognisable body behind. As I continued lifting, I remember seeing Si running as fast as his legs could carry him. He knelt at my side, and I tried everything in my power to return into my lifeless body – but no matter how hard I tried, I could not return. Instead, I rose higher and higher. I remember thinking, *Why could I not have been allowed to stay until I told Si how much I loved him?* You know, like what happens in the movies and stuff.'

I nod. 'Wow, Syd, how very sad … but you must be so proud of yourself, though. You're a hero.'

'I suppose I should be, Roo, but I'm not. It was reckless of me to have intervened in fate.'

'What do you mean? I don't understand.'

'Let me put it like this. The elderly gentleman I saved was eighty-six. It was his time to move on from this world, and this was how it was planned for him … his "calling", so to speak. Sure, after he witnessed what had occurred as a result of his stupidity, he had a heart attack and died on the pavement beside me. He was going to die, anyway; but because I intervened, I was also taken when I shouldn't have been. When I arrived at the gates of Heaven, there was no place reserved for me. Actually, my place was reserved for when I was eighty-two. I would have had a great life … if only I had not played the superhero! Now I'll miss out on all the things I planned – marrying Si, having kids and even being a granny, for that matter.'

'So, why did you end up in the Waiting Zone? Why didn't they just send you back if it was not your time to die?'

'I asked Boss that when I first met him. He explained that people like me – people who die before getting to live their lives to the full – provide the very gifts that we in the Waiting Zone work to deliver. That's why we do the gem test first, because the gifts are truly that – each one is a "gift" – they are special and not to be given to just anyone. They are gifts that have to be earned, as what they produce are special children with big hearts and minds, who will grow into people willing to help others without question. But to their advantage they also have a built-in awareness control that enables them to foresee danger so they will never come to any harm until it is their time to move on.'

'Wow, Syd! Why did I not know all of this?'

'I suppose you never asked Boss, did you?'

'No, I didn't. I also arrived here because I shouldn't have died when I did. I wonder if the gift I produced has ever been used. I suppose that's something I will never discover.'

We both sit in silence for a few moments, each engaged in our own deep thoughts.

'How many years do you have left to wait, Syd?'

'Thirty-eight years, Roo. And then I can move on.'

'Well, I hope Si will be there waiting for you.'

'He won't be waiting for me.'

'How do you knowt hat? He might be …'

'He got on with his life, Roo. He met someone else and they've had five children together. He has a big family, and I'm just a distant memory for him. I often dream about what my life would have been like had it not ended so early. I would have what his wife has now: plenty of children and love. But I also know I haveto move on, too, as it would drive me crazy to think about it too much.'

'Well, Syd, if I enter Heaven before you, I'll wait at the gates for you to enter.'

'That's very kind of you. I really appreciate that you would do that for me.'

She leans over and gives me a kiss on the cheek, and I feel a spark that I haven't felt in a long time. We look deep into each other's eyes, naturally entering each other's souls to see what we can find there. It is an intensely intimate experience.

This shakes me up, as I feel that I am being unfaithful to Josie. I speak to break the connection between us. 'Anyway, what do you suggest we do about Jayden? He's gone too far and he mustn't get away with it.'

Syd looks at me for a moment before she answers. 'Yes. Well, I have a plan.'

'You certainly come prepared, I'll give you that – no hanging about where you're concerned.'

'You have to be in this game, Roo. Sure, look at what Jayden did and how he expects to get away with it! My plan is simple: we've-discovered what's happened here, so we can manage the situation. The way we deal with it depends on who has received the gift. What do you think?'

'Great minds think alike! How about this: we do a quick check of my recipients, and if they react as expected to the news they're expecting, we decide if they should be allowed to keep the gift. Then we can contact Boss to fill him in.'

'He isn't going to behappy.'

'No, of course he isn't, but once we explain what Jayden did – and how we have been trying to sort it out with as little upheaval as possible – I'm sure he will understand.'

'I suppose so … and hopefully he will sort Jayden out.'

'Right … let's see who got the first gem. Oh, yes, it was Siobhan; she conceived it with some young law student she is mentoring. I don't think a child has first priority in her future plans but, hey, the gems are supposed to stop the recipients in their tracks and make them think. Siobhan could surprise us, but I don't feel she is ready for a child. The process has not begun for her … not yet, anyway.'

'Yeah, I agree. Who's next?'

'Bethany. She is such a gorgeous girl, on the inside as well as on the outside. She's quite young and she's hoping her actor boyfriend will ask her to marry him. She's been through a high-pressure childhood, with her mum being so pushy and all … treating her as if she were a little display doll. It will be interesting to see how she reacts to her news.'

'Tracy was next, wasn't she? I would so love for her to be the one who has received the true gift, because I don't think she will deal well with another loss. Life can be so cruel sometimes.'

'Yeah, Tracy has had it hard and it would be great for us if it was her. It would be easier to go to Boss knowing it was Tracy who received the true gift … as if a miracle occurred. This is a plausible explanation, I think.'

'Yes … very plausible. Wasn't Kath next? Wow! She went through a time of it during her teens, didn't she? But she's still a good person.It's a pity she never found love and settled down before now, but maybe the insecurities stemming from her baby being taken away meant she was always afraid to take the chance of it happening again.'

I nod. 'Last but not least was Carrie. I was surprised I needed to intervene with a crystal to instigate enough of a connection for them toget to a place where they would share their love for one another. I don't feel it would be a good time for a new baby to enter their lives. Carrie still needs a helping hand to guide her towards her full emotional and spiritual restoration – that violent incident shocked her to her core, and she needs to emerge from survival mode in order to be ready for another child. Her body and mind have protected themselves effectively by going into shock – and luckily she understood what was going on, listened to her body and took her recovery one day at a time. But it's now time for her to move forward in her spiritual journey of self-discovery so she can reach a better place of positivity, peace and forgiveness within; this will ultimately bring her to a place of spiritual happiness for the rest of her life … and beyond. I know I keep saying it, but if only she knew now how happy she is going to be in her future.'

'I know exactly what you mean, Roo. Sometimes when we feel we have gone as low as we possibly can, it is actually a good thing because we all have the power to rise from that dark and depressing place. When we do, we are always wiser and more aware of true happiness as a result of embarking on our own private voyage of self-discovery. We emerge more in tune with ourselves and more in control of our reactions. We are able to look at life from a totally different perspective than before, and that can only be a good thing.'

We stayed on the hill all night long, gazing at the stars, not saying a word. Syd and I know each other so well that we can do this often; we do not need words because we know each other's thoughts. We work so well together. Boss knew exactly what he was doing when he teamed us up: she looks out for me and I look out for her – that's why I promised I would wait for her at the gates if my gift is planted first. Syd and I have stuck together through thick and thin over the past thirty-four years, and if it were the case that I had no-one waiting for me, I would want her to wait for me at the gates, too. However, that will not happen because when my gift is planted, I will enter the gates to live eternally in divine happiness with my Josie and our child.

Chapter Twelve

Positive Results

We have used our time-travelling capabilities to accelerate six weeks into the future. I didn't like using this feature when I first started this job, but I soon realised how valuable an asset it is. Syd has decided to stick with me so we can assess the situation together. I am quite glad to have her moral support. I would do exactly the same for her, and I think she knows that – I certainly hope she does.

Back to the task at hand. The process of deciding which three of the five women should receive the gift is sometimes hard; we must carry out a thorough assessment, as we are dealing with people's future happiness. In a sense, we are playing God as we determine the outcome, thereby quite possibly changing the fate of these women and their families.

So, with a fresh, clear, revitalised mind, I will now embark on the duty of observing the reactions.

TRACY

I visit Tracy first. It has been six weeks since I released her gem, so she should be feeling some changes already. When I arrive, I see that she is still in bed. Rob has come into the bedroom holding a tray.

'Thanks, love, but I'm not hungry.'

'You have to keep your strength up.'

'I need to get up, Rob. It's not good for Joey to see me just lying about. Anyway, you have to go to work.'

'Don't worry about Joey, love. I'm going to take him for a walk to the park, and as for work, I've taken the rest of the week off.'

'Yes, but …'

'Yes, but nothing … I was due some holidays anyway, so I am at your service.'

She starts to cry and he hurries to her side. 'Hey, what's wrong? You should be happy, love.'

'Yes, I know … But what if it happens again, Rob? I don't think I could stand it.'

'If it happens again, it just wasn't meant to be, love. It would mean something was wrong, and so it would be for the best, as its quality of life would not be the best.'

'Thanks for being my rock, Rob. This should be a joyously happy time for us, and I'm ruining it by being like this but I can't help how I feel.'

'Listen, love, some things are out of our control. We just need to deal with them the best we can and try to get on with things, but it does no harm to be cautious, either.'

Giving her a kiss on the forehead, he gets up to leave the room. He stops in the doorway, turns towards her and says, 'Now make sure you get some rest, love. I'll be back in an hour or so. Do you want anything before I go?'

'I'm okay; make sure that Joey doesn't try to run away.'

Tracy is obviously nervous about the prospect of miscarrying; if she does, it will hit her the hardest, I believe, as she wants this baby so much. Still, everything happens for a reason – and the outcome of that is for the greater good of the person and the people closest to that person.

CARRIE

I move on to visit Carrie. She is inside the cottage; the windows are small, and she does not have a light on, so the visibility is not great. Tom has just gone out the door and she has rushed to the bedroom, where she looks in the side pocket of a large bag. She has pulled out a pregnancy test that seems to have been in the bag a while.She checks on her son; he is having a nap and looks peaceful. She strokes his face lovingly with her finger, then goes to the toilet to conduct the test.

When she comes out, she looks quite pale. She is shaking a little as she holds the stick up to the light. Opening the front door, she sticks her head out and calls Tom back to the house.

'What's up? You look like you've just seen a ghost.'

'Here, take a look at this, will you …?'

She hands him the stick and he looks at it, not comprehending.

'What is it?'

'It's a pregnancy test, Tom. I'm pregnant.'

'Oh, but that's good … right?' he asks her cautiously as an inner glow starts to beam from his very core.

'Well, I don't know, Tom … I was gonna ask you the same thing.'

'I'm happy about it if you are.'

'Yeah, I think I am. I just never thought about us having another one. Have you?'

'To be honest, yes. I'd love another child, but I wasn't sure that you wanted to, Carrie.'

'I might pop into the chemist to get another test … just to be sure. Can you stay here with Max? He's still asleep.'

'Yeah, sure. Go on ahead, darling.'

He gives her a loving kiss as she goes out the door. He saw she was shaking from the shock of it all and it was an 'I am so happy that we are having another child' kind of kiss. I wait to continue my observations.

Carrie returns a half an hour later, still shaking, and completes a second test, which is also positive. When she shows Tom the results, he smiles with deep joy – he wouldn't care if the whole world fell in around him. From his spot in a chair, he pulls her down onto his knee and hugs her. She beams him a smile, looking as though she could not be happier about anything than feeling his warmth again. They sit there in each other's arms until Max wakes.

Carrie knows it will all be okay. Things seem to be coming together here; the gem is doing its job well. I am relieved that my intervention with the crystal seems to have turned out for the best.

BETHANY

I go to the city next, visiting Bethany's apartment first. I go in to discover her in the bathroom with her head over the toilet bowl. She is heaving her stomach out, poor thing.

'Are you okay, Beth?' asks Hanson.

'I'll be out in a minute, I'm not feeling … *ugh!*'

'Can I get you anything? Do you want me to call your agent?'

She cleans herself up and comes out of the bathroom.

'Sorry, hon, I just couldn't stop it. I must have eaten something dodgy last night.'

'But, Beth, we both had the same things to eat, and I feel fine. I think you'd better make an appointment with the doc.'

'I don't have time to do that today. I'll try to get in tomorrow.'

'If you don't call, I will! You cannot go another day like this – you'll waste away on me.'

'Okay. I'll ring before I leave, I promise.'

'And you will let me know what he says straightaway, won't you?'

'Yes, of course I will. I don't want you worrying any longer than necessary.'

He kisses her on the cheek and rushes out the door. Sure enough, she rings the doctors to see if they have any cancellations; they have an 11:30 slot, which she books. She texts Hanson to let him know.

She arrives at the doctor's office, where the usual scurries of people approach her, asking for pictures and autographs. Luckily, she is called almost immediately.

'Hello, Bethany. How can I help you today?'

'Well, it's just that I haven't been feeling very well lately, Doctor. I was wondering if I've caught a bug or something.'

'How long have you been feeling unwell?'

'I wasn't feeling too well yesterday, but it's worse today. I have been getting sick all morning, and Hanson made me promise to come see you.'

'Would you be able to do a sample of urine?'

'Oh, yes, I suppose I could.'

'Good. Take this for the sample. The toilet is the second door on your left; just come back here when you're done.'

She takes the little plastic bottle from his hand, goes to the toilet and completes the task. Once back in the room, she takes her seat again. The doctor conducts the necessary urine tests and then he sits down at his desk, facing her.

'Bethany, have you ever considered that you might be pregnant?'

'Well, no, Doctor. We always use protection. I couldn't afford to … *oh* … you mean …?'

'Yes, my dear, you are pregnant. How do you feel about that?'

'Erm … I don't really know … I've never thought about it before … This is a bit of a shock, to tell you the truth, Doctor.'

'I can understand that, dear. Take a few minutes to let yourself absorb it if you like. Do you think Hanson will be pleased?'

'Oh, yes, Hanson … I don't know … we're not married or anything … we hadn't really talked about starting a family.'

'Is there anyone you can talk to about this at the moment? Would you like me to call Hanson to come pick you up?'

'No, no … I'll be okay. I'll just go home and wait for him; it will give me a chance to think.'

'Are you sure? Because I can ask one of the nurses to make you a nice cup of tea, and you can have a little chat with her …'

'Thanks very much, Doctor, but I think it will be fine. Goodbye, Doctor.'

'Goodbye, Beth. You know where we are if you need us.'

She politely leaves the room.

She goes home and sits by the window, staring at the city below. Her mobile rings constantly with calls from Hanson and her agent. Yet she doesn't even flinch at the sounds; she stares ahead and rocks slowly back and forth in a desperate attempt to comfort herself.

Hanson rushes into the apartment to see her sitting in the dark; she doesn't move an inch after his dramatic burst into the room like an all-time superhero. He switches on a light and runs straight over to her.

'Beth, what is it? What's wrong, my princess? I've been so worried all day!'

She still doesn't answer; it is as if she doesn't even know he is standing there.

'Beth, come on … you're killing me here. Please! Was it something the doc said? Are you very ill? Please, Beth, just tell me, and then I can help.'

'He said … he said I'm pregnant. I'm sorry, Hanson. I didn't mean for it to happen…'

He picks her up in his arms as though he were carrying her over the threshold.

'Oh, Beth! That's wonderful news! You'll just have to marry me now.'

Those words seem to bring her back to life. 'What did you just say?' she asks.

He sets her on her feet, ever so gently.

'Just stand there a minute, Beth … don't move.'

He rushes off, coming back to her side just as quickly, and then he gets down on one knee.

'Bethany Georgina Moore, will you please do me the honour of becoming my wife?'

Lovingly, he gazes up into her eyes and opens a little black velvet box that he has clutched in his hand. The diamond ring he reveals is like no other I have seen; a real sparkler, for sure.

'Yes, Hanson Murdoch Jones, I would love to be your wife.'

He kisses her tummy, stands up and then picks her up again, swinging her around joyfully. Suddenly he stops, saying, 'Oh, sorry, Beth! I shouldn't have done that … are you okay?'

'I'm fine. Do it again!'

So he does, and then he carries her to their oversized sofa, where he sits down, cradling her in his arms and kissing her tenderly.

'Thank you for making me the happiest man on Earth.'

'You're very welcome. I have to admit that I am kind of chuffed myself. I didn't know you wanted kids.'

'I've been planning to ask you to marry me for a while now – that's why I had the ring at the ready – but the right moment just never seemed to arise. We were both too busy … working all the time. I would love nothing more than to slow life down and have some children with you. You will be a wonderful mum.'

Those are the words she has needed to hear. She has resisted bringing a child into the world, not wanting to make any little one as miserable as her mum made her.

'You do know there is going to be a lot of publicity about this, Hanson. Let's not tell anyone about the baby yet. I'd like to save something for us to treasure without those reporters making judgements about us, and I don't want my mum to know yet, either. You know what she's like; she'll try to control everything – I just couldn't stand it.'

'You really have to start standing up to her, Beth. You are your own person and she doesn't own you. You should sack her as your agent.'

'I know you're right, and I will do it. But we have more important things to deal with right now.'

She puts her hand on her tummy, and he places his hand over hers. They gaze into each other's eyes without saying another word.

The gem has made dramatic progress here. It is strange how her first reaction was that being pregnant was a bad thing. Her mother obviously instilled a lot of her own beliefs into this young woman, not allowing her to make decisions or have her own views when she was younger, forcing her to comply with whatever her mum thought was best.

But Bethany has begun to realise she can make decisions on

her own and no longer needs to be under her mum's control. She is going to be a mum herself and that has made her stronger; she has more to think about than just herself, and there is no way in the world she is going to let her mum dictate what she does with her child – in fact, she probably will not allow her to have anything to do with the baby at all.

I will leave Bethany at this point, as I believe the gem has done its job. Bethany has covered a lot of ground; her life is moving quickly now, and it is in the direction she chooses and feels comfortable with.

KATH

Kath, too, is about to discover her news. She is in a gymnasium doing a fitness class with her Energisers. She isn't feeling so well, and the class notices she doesn't seem to have her usual motivational energy. She stops for a moment to gather herself together because she is feeling quite dizzy.

'I am so sorry about this, I've come over all dizzy,' she apologises. 'I need a moment to compose myself.'

One of the other women rushes up to Kath and hands her a bottle of water.

'Thank you ...' Kath manages, but before she can say more, she passes out.

Someone calls an ambulance, and the paramedics bring her round. In the distance, she sees her Energisers looking on, concerned, so she tries to get up.

'Sorry, lovey,' one of the paramedics says. 'I need you to lie here until we find out what's wrong.'

'But I'm feeling fine now, thanks ... really, I promise.'

'I'm sure you are, lovey, but you didn't faint for no reason, and it's my job to discover that reason. Your blood pressure is a bit high; have you been under any stress lately?'

'No, nothing out of the ordinary.'

'Have you been eating properly? How have you been feeling generally?'

'Now that you mention it, I have been feeling a little extra tired. And I'm off my food, as the prospect of eating, especially first thing in the morning, makes me feel quite nauseated.'

'Is there any chance you're pregnant?'

This question takes Kath by surprise, drawing her straight back to her teen years – she remembers the school nurse asking her the same question.

'No, I am definitely not pregnant. There would be no chance … no chance at all.'

The paramedic, immediately picking up on Kath's defensiveness, replies, 'Oh, right. Okay. Standard question.'

'Can I go now?'

'I am sorry, lovey, but you won't be able to go anywhere for a while. I'm going to have to bring you in for some tests so we can eliminate some of the worst-case scenarios.'

So they bring her out on a stretcher to the ambulance. Kath finds it an embarrassing experience, further enhanced by the large number of photographers waiting outside to get shots for the media. In the hospital, they do some blood tests and Kath needs to wait for the results before they will discharge her.

She lies in her hospital bed in a little private room, reading a magazine. She looks up when she hears the door open, and to her surprise, it's James. She can hardly believe it, but there he is, holding a bunch of flowers that he obviously bought at a garage along the way.

'How did you know I was here?' she asks. Her tone sounds

accusing, but she doesn't mean it to.

He takes it in stride. 'Well, I heard on the radio that you had collapsed in one of your classes. I was worried, so I rushed over. They only let me in because I said I was your husband.'

She melts a bit and then giggles. 'You didn't … did you?'

He grins. 'Are you okay, Kath?'

'They don't know what's wrong yet, but they're waiting for test results to come so they can give me the all clear to go.'

At that moment, the doctor enters the room. 'Kath, we have the results of your tests. I am glad to tell you that we know what is wrong with you.'

He looks over at James as if he expects him to leave.

'Don't worry about him, Doctor. I will be telling him anyway. What is it? What's wrong with me?'

'Well, Kath, you are pregnant.'

'I am … what? That can't be possible, Doctor. Are you sure you haven't made a mistake?'

'Sure, I'm sure. We will just check your vitals and then you will be free to go.'

Kath sits in a daze.

'Kath, are you feeling okay?' James' voice is full of concern. 'You seem a bit … shocked.'

'Of course I'm shocked, James! Surely you didn't plan for this to happen to us again.'

'No, of course I didn't plan it! But you can't compare it to the last time. We were only kids and your parents took over. It can be different this time, Kath, we can do this. We can do it together.'

'But I have my career to think of.'

'You're just looking for excuses. It's happened, and we're going to have to work it out together.'

'I need to think things through, James. Do you mind giving me a lift home?'

So she is not alone this time; if things had been different twenty-two years ago, I believe these two could have made it work, even as young as they were at the time. If they'd had the support of their families, instead of the intervention that took place and ruined so many lives, I think Kath and James could have worked it out. I will be interested to see how this progresses.

SIOBHAN

I visit Siobhan last. I have been good, as I have purposefully stopped myself from making any judgements as to how she will react to her news. I can only pray she has not received the gift, because I feel that would be the worst possible result at this time – but there I go again, being judgemental …

Today, as she storms through the building, it is not hard to see that she is not her usual self. Her hair is not brushed and her make-up is incomplete. Her usual welcoming committee are taken aback, barely able to get out the usual, 'Good Morning, Miss Roe', so shocked are they by the sight of her unkempt appearance at this early hour. However, they are relieved to avoid the torrent of abuse that usually flies their way while they just try to get on with their jobs.

When she reaches her office thirty minutes late, her assistant is keen to help her, clearly concerned by the disturbing sight that confronts her.

'Miss Roe, is everything okay? You look terrible.'

'I know, Bea. I feel terrible, but I have to be in the high court in an hour.'

'What can I do to help? Do you want a coffee?'

'Erm, no, I had better not. A glass of ice water would be good, thanks.'

Bea is not used to her boss talking civilly to her, but she is keen to help and doesn't wonder about it too much.

'I have a friend down the street who is a hairdresser, Miss Roe. Would you like me to ask her to call up here?'

'My hair … oh, yes, my hair … it must look a dreadful sight … yes, would you, Bea? That would be great.'

So Bea goes off to get a glass of water and to phone her friend.

When she returns, Siobhan tells her, 'Hold my calls, Bea, and I don't want to see anyone today, either. Okay?'

'No-one at all? Are you sure, Miss Roe?'

'Yes, Bea. No-one. I am quite sure.'

'Okay, Miss Roe, just call me if you need anything.'

Bea quickly leaves the room to call her friend on the bottom floor, who informs her that Siobhan's condition has turned out to be the topic of the day at Maximus Corporation.

The buzzer goes on Siobhan's telephone.

'Miss Roe, Will is here, and he says he needs to see you urgently …'

'Let him in, Bea,' Siobhan says quickly before Bea can ask why she's changed her mind about having no visitors.

Will enters Siobhan's office, which is quite dark; she has the blind tightly closed and no lights are on.

'What's going on, Siobhan? The whole building is talking about you! They're saying you're having some sort of breakdown … Gee, you really don't look well. Are you sick?'

'Well, you could say that, Will. I just have a few things I need to sort out. Do you mind giving me some space to do that?'

'I will, if you explain what's going on.'

'Why? So that you can go and share it with your comrades on the bottom floor? I don't think so.'

'Siobhan, you know that I would never talk about us! What we do is between us – just you and me – and whatever anyone else says is just speculation … You know that, right?'

'No, I don't know that, Will, but what I do know is that I have a lot of sorting out to do and you are not helping by pushing me at the moment.'

'I take it tonight is cancelled, then?'

'Oh, just get out, Will! Is that all you think about?'

She pushes him out the door, watching him shrug his shoulders at Bea on the way past. She knows she could never share her news with him. He is her plaything. He is not in it for the long haul, he is just trying to sleep his way to the top – just like she did.

She closes the door, goes back to her desk, sits in her chair and sighs. With her head in the palms of her hands, she says, 'Dear Lord, why me? Why now? I don't think I'm ready; how will I make a good mum?'

And then she cries. This is not a reaction I expected from her.

Ever since she learned her news, her attitude has completely changed. I feel potential here, as she seems to have dramatically taken her head out of the clouds and come back down to Earth. The fact she is not conscious of her appearance indicates she is having an inner conflict; she is dealing with issues she has kept covered up for a long time. With conflict comes change, and the first thing that has changed is the tough-guy act she puts so much effort into portraying. Now she has exposed herself as not being so totally in control – not nearly as tough as she wants others to think she is – and I believe that, over time, she will discover she receives a better response from others when she is being herself.

Different people react differently to the news they are going to have a 'new addition'; some reactions are physical and some are psychological. All these changes are necessary in order to prepare a woman to be more resilient during her pregnancy. My advice to women is simple: listen to yourself. If you need to be sick, be sick; if you need to cry, go ahead and cry; if you are doing too much, your body will respond by shutting itself down for a time, and you may faint. The body truly is a wonderful thing.

Chapter Thirteen
Summoned

Syd has viewed all that I have of the five different women and now she and I need to assess our observations. We have decided to go back to our hilltop spot and have a picnic. We set it up and it looks picture perfect – complete with a checkered picnic blanket and a wicker basket. She really knows how to do things, does Syd. I have always admired her for the effort she takes; over the years, she has really gone out of her way to put on some great bashes.

We don't celebrate birthdays in the Waiting Zone, as none of us age here; we stay the age we were when we arrived. We measure time by the number of years of service we have completed. Obviously, the older you are when you enter, the shorter the period of time you will have to remain in the Waiting Zone, as you have arrived closer to the time for your intended entrance into Heaven. Syd's and my lives were cut short unnecessarily, so we both have longer to wait. In short, our gifts are not yet ready to return to the world.

When I arrived in the Waiting Zone I was in a state of confusion as I searched for my Josie, desperate to be reunited with her and our newborn. I was convinced the physical pain I felt deep within because of losing them would never be relieved until the three of us were reunited. However, since then, while doing my job in the Waiting Zone, I have discovered that time is a great healer.

And not just time. Syd has helped me tremendously, too. From the time I arrived, she has always been there for me: she let me talk, and she listened. She was my shoulder to cry on when the realisation hit me that things could never be the same again. She helped me come to terms with the changes that had consumed my life as it was. We have been close friends ever since, and I have come to see that it is as if we were destined to meet. I hold our friendship so dear to my heart, and I know that, without Syd, my stay in the Waiting Zone would have been more of a challenge.

Over the past thirty-four years, Syd has always gone out of her way for me. Each year on the anniversary of the day I entered the Waiting Zone, she has thrown a 'surprise party' for me. She goes to such lengths and puts forth such effort every year to disguise the fact that she is organising a party – and I go to such lengths and put forth such effort every year to pretend I don't know what is going on. It is quite comical really, and such fun too, now that I really think about it, which I haven't over the years. We are like one of those old married couples, so content when we are with each other, and there is nothing we don't know about each other now that Syd has told me the story of how she entered the Waiting Zone. In all those years we have been practically inseparable. Syd and I truly are the closest of friends. Why am I just now realising all this?

I am seeing her in a totally different light. I watch as she sets up the picnic with such attention to detail; any party organiser would be proud to do as well. Everything she does, she does with style and class; she truly is wonderful, and I have just recognised that …

Syd and I are comrades in our quest to give the true gifts to those worthy of receiving them. We have always made great decisions together, as our minds think alike, even though our characters are different.

Syd's message connector beeps, and she shoots right uplike a lightning bolt. In that instant it happens – what I have dreaded ever since Syd told me about Jayden's trickery.

'Uh-oh.'

'What? What is it, Syd?'

'Boss is looking for me, and for you, too, I believe.'

My connector beeps. It is a message from Boss: *Need you to come back to base ASAP.*

I look at Syd. 'Yeah, I just got summoned, too. Will we go together?'

'Sure, Roo, we may as well … what have we got to lose? At least we can support each other.'

'What about our picnic?'

'And what do we tell Boss when we arrive in the zone late, Roo? "Sorry we're late, Boss, we finished our picnic lunch first." I don't think so.' Syd pulls a face.

She's right, as usual. I shrug. 'Well, we had better get a move on.'

We head to the Vortex. I didn't expect to be back here so soon. We knock on the door to Boss' office, and it suddenly opens itself. Syd and I nervously walk in and approach the desk, which looks the same as ever – large and white and very tidy, indeed.

The grand white leather swivel chair is facing the wall. All of a sudden, the chair swings around to reveal Boss, sitting with his legs crossed and his hands together.

'Well? Have you anything that you need to fill me in on?' he asks.

Syd and I look from one to the other, neither wanting to be the one to tell him.

I eventually speak because it's Syd who is helping me so I need to step up.

'I am sorry, Boss. I've only just discovered the problem myself. Syd messaged me after I had released the gems.'

'What problem?'

I hesitate. 'You summoned us, Boss ... is it because a gift has been released?'

'Yes, Rupert. I know all about it. Jayden visited me to inform me that you had taken a gift.'

'But I didn't just take it, Boss! He tricked me.' I feel well within my rights to defend myself.

'Rupert, I have known about this all along; I do get alerted every time a gift is released. I have checked the records, so I know the gift was released before you entered dispatch. I also understand that Jayden has been creating a few problems for you lately.'

'Yes, well, I know he wants my job, Boss. He's made it quite clear that he wants to be the Visitor, but I don't think he has the qualities,' I say boldly.

Syd finally pipes up in my defence. 'Yeah, Boss, it's not Roo's fault.'

'Ah, thanks, Syd. You really jumped to my defence there – better late than never,' I say in a low voice. After all she's done for me, I suppose I could have suppressed the sarcasm, but I'm in quite a state.

'Yes, thank you, Sydney. I do know that; I take it all into account. Would you please wait outside for a few moments while I talk to Rupert?'

Before she leaves the room, she turns and whispers in my ear. 'I'm just outside, Roo, call if you need me.'

I certainly do not know what to expect. Boss usually likes an audience when he gives us a drilling.

'Rupert, you know how the Waiting Zone works: we are here until our gifts are released; the release of our gifts is our "ticket" to the gates of Heaven, so to speak.'

'Yes, Boss, I understand that clearly.' I do not tell him I did not see the full picture until my recent talk with Syd. 'I have been waiting thirty-four years to earn that right so I can be reunited with my wife and child.'

'I must inform you that it was your gift that has been released, which means that, after this assignment, you will be free to enter Heaven.'

This takes me aback, and I fall into the seat behind me. 'Are you sure, Boss?'

'Yes, Rupert. One of the women is carrying your gift.'

'I just can't believe it … I have waited so long for this moment and yet it is all quite surreal … I don't know how I feel. Do you know who has received the gift?'

'Now, Rupert, you know I cannot tell you that, even if I wanted to. You will find out soon enough.'

'Okay, fair enough, Boss. Can I go absorb it all?'

'Yes, surely. But, before you go, I want to share something with you.'

He leans forward in the chair,resting his hands on the desk. There is a warm expression on his face that I have never seen before.

'As you already know, I have been the Boss here since you arrived. I started the position many years before you came. I entered the

Waiting Zone under circumstances similar to your own; I, too, was assigned the role of Visitor.'

'You were once a Visitor?' I ask, utterly surprised.

'Yes, Rupert, I was. That may be hard for you to imagine, but like yourself, I took my role very seriously – in fact, I see some of myself in you. When my time to enter Heaven came, I arrived at the gates only to discover that nobody was there to meet me. My wife had not passed on, and it was probably quite a number of years before she was going to do so. I was alone, and I missed the Waiting Zone and the life I had built up here. I was given the opportunity to return as the Boss because the previous Boss had seen potential in me, and he felt it was the right time for him to move on to Heaven as the arrival time of his loved ones drew nearer.' He paused and studied me. 'Do you understand what I am saying, Rupert?'

'Yes, Boss, that is a very touching story. I don't want to be rude, but I don't know what it has to do with me.'

'That's fine, I just wanted to share it with you, is all. You are free to go, and I hope that you and Sydney have a lovely picnic.'

'Oh. So you know just about everything, right?'

'Right,' he says, smiling.

I smile back, realising that Boss has known every single thing I have done over the past thirty-four years – and not only everything I have done, but everything everyone else has done, too. I can't wait to tell Syd!

As I exit the office, she rushes towards me. Throwing her arms around me, she exclaims, 'Please tell me you aren't going to be sacked as Visitor, Roo! Tell me that Jayden is not going to take your place – I simply couldn't bear it.'

'No, Syd, nothing of the sort. Where did you get that idea from? You have been thinking worst-case scenarios again, haven't you?'

'It prepares me for the worst possible outcome and it works for me. So what did he say?'

'I'm so excited! Boss told me my gift has been released. This is my last assignment as the Visitor – how great is that?'

Syd releases me from the embrace. All the colour drains from her face as she absorbs the realisation I will be leaving.

'Oh, Syd, I'm sorry. I was so wrapped up in my own joy, I didn't even consider that you might be upset.'

'I'm fine, Roo. It's unexpected, that's all. I thought you and I would be here working together longer. But I'm just being silly.' She beams me a smile. 'So you are finally going to be reunited with Josie – how exciting for you!'

I grin. 'Well, Boss said for us to have a lovely picnic. Do you fancy picking up where we left off before we were summoned?'

'Sure, why not.'

I fill her in on what I recently learned about Boss's omniscience as we head back through dispatch.

Jayden is still there, which I find strange. Boss knew what he had done and was aware of the circumstances. It was a serious offence, and Jayden should not still be in a position where he has control over the gifts; they are too precious for him to be messing about with them.

A realisation suddenly hits me: How did Jayden know which gift was mine to plant?

As I pass his desk, he looks up at me. I stare at him coldlyto let him know that I know what he did. It doesn't seem to bother him, though, as he smiles and goes on with his work. It is strange that he didn't comment, but I shrug it off – maybe he has decided to mend his ways. One can only hope …

But I am not going to let Jayden ruin my happiness at knowing my reunion with Josie and our child is so close; nor am I going to waste any time I have left to spend with Syd. I shall miss my dear friend sorely.

Chapter Fourteen

Attaining the Gems

This is the part of my job that I do not enjoy. But, alas, it must be done in order for my assignment to be complete. It is by observing each woman at this point that I get a true picture of the depth of her desire to have a child. For some reason, it is even harder than usual this time. I wish Syd were here to observe with me, but she has had to go back to the Waiting Zone. We have arranged to meet later to discuss my observations of the five women.

Perhaps it is more difficult because this is my last assignment; I will enter Heaven before long. I am ecstatic at the thought of eternal happiness with Josie and our child. But I cannot allow my mind to wander – I must focus on the task at hand, complete my assignment and then be on my way. Forcing my mind back to the five women I must observe, I consider what I have learned during my time as Visitor.

Life sometimes grants wisdom in mysterious ways: to enable us to reach the tranquility of the destination, we must endure some pain on the journey – but ultimately, the pain is worth enduring, as most people will agree at the end. To appreciate the true wealth in life, such as the gift of life, we sometimes need to be brought back from a place that values materialistic gain over the gift of life. This process of balancing values takes time to complete, and the time varies from person to person.

However, people who have experienced the process and achieved true balance always feel happier within, more satisfied with life and more comfortable in their own skin. This voyage of self-discovery grounds people, cementing each brick of their lives together, so they are able to build secure and stable lives. As they have now built the foundations which will enable all their succeeding bricks to stand tall, proud and secure among those already in place.

Those people who take the time to build sturdy foundations will discover they are more secure and better able to withstand the 'surprises' of life, such as when an Earth-shattering moment occurs. They will discover their life's structure will not fall to the ground; it may sway and be shaken, but it will still be secure after the dramatic event.

When the gem comes, it is like an earthquake for those it visits, shaking them to the core; but if they have secure life foundations, they will be stronger when the effects of the personal trauma have stopped rippling through their every thought. However, some people are built of steel and they may not feel any ripples at all – this is unfortunate, as they will miss out on the grounding natural realities that come with life.

I prepare myself to call the gems. I stand on the highest point of the tallest mountain and open the box that sends out a signal that summons the precious gems back to where they belong. The signal is so intense that it causes lights to flicker all over the world. The first gem races towards me: it is as bright as the sun and as beautiful as only a gem can be. It shines brightly in the sky, radiating all the colours of the rainbow as it speeds along. Should you ever see a rainbow when there has been no rain, you will know a gem is returning home.

One by one, they return, each one creating a spectacular scene as it zooms through the fluffy white clouds until it reaches the destination of its sanctuary: the treasure box. The speed at which each one comes is so fast, its journey is but a blur of colour; and then, just as quickly, each one stops and hovers above its allocated spot. Five were released, but only four have returned, so I know for sure that a gift has been released … just as Boss assured me.

This time is different from any other time, as I know the gift released was my own. I am tempted to peek in order to see which of the five women has received it, but I know I am not yet ready to discover that. It might affect me and any judgements I make during the last stage.

I will complete my assignment in the standard manner, by observing each of the five women for the last time. The main objective is to see how they deal with the loss and how deeply they desire to have a child, as I already started to explain. This is important because the gifts we distribute from the Waiting Zone are priceless: children born from gifts are special and will exceed any expectations because of their knowledge and self-awareness. The high value they place on life will be so strong that their positivity will spill onto others who have the pleasure of their company. Their aura is white, which represents an angelically spiritual person who also incorporates the good qualities from each of the other aura colours.

The courier comes to pick up the gems. I meet him at the entrance to the Vortex. He is tall and does not have much meat on his bones. His brown hair looks as though his mother licked her hand and patted it down. He always wears a brown uniform: a pair of trousers (which are way too tight, and someone should inform him about that); a jacket that cuts off at the waist, and that has breast pockets and a zip that he never fails to have zipped up halfway, revealing a beige shirt that opens at the collar.

'Hi, Rupert. I believe you're leaving us,' he says in greeting.

'News sure travels fast in the zone, Jake.'

'You know how it goes – once it's in the system, everyone knows about it. What's this I hear about a missing gem?'

'Yeah, there are only four gems to collect because one was a gift, and we all know that gifts don't return unless they are terminated.'

'Wow! You're having a ball down here on this assignment, aren't ya?'

'You know me, Jake … I like to keep things interesting.'

'Okay, mate, I'll let ya get back to it. I'll probably see you at your leaving party.'

'What leaving party?'

'Ah, don't let on you don't know. Sure, hasn't Syd organised a party for you every year since you came? Do you think she's going to miss an opportunity to organise your leaving party? Either she has a thing about parties or she is really crazy about you … I know which one I'd put my bets on, you lucky guy!'

'Come on, Jake. Syd and I are just good friends.'

'Yeah, yeah. I've heard that one before.'

I wave him off and he takes the treasure box.

There is nothing Jake likes more than a bit of gossip. He is the courier, after all. He is so suited to his job, as he not only delivers and collects goods, but also spreads good and bad news.

Can a man and a woman not simply have a friendship? In some

people's eyes it is not possible. They believe the laws of attraction will intervene at some point – because, obviously, some attraction must exist in order to enable friends of the opposite sex to spend so much time together. I do acknowledge this, but I still say it is possible for a man and a woman to 'just be friends'. Syd and I have been friends – good friends – for thirty-four years, we hardly ever fight, and we have never been intimate – well, apart from one kiss, but that was nothing …

TRACY

I put all that out of my head. I must complete my assignment. This is the penultimate moment, and I need to focus all my powers of concentration on each of the five women so I can conduct an honest final observation.

I visit Tracy first. This poor woman and her family have been through the mill, and now I have added to it. I enter her home to see her in tears, desperately pressing the numbers in the telephone handset. Her son, Joey, is in the living room, watching *Tom and Jerry* cartoons. She puts the phone to her ear, sits down and buries her face in her free hand.

'Rob … it's happened again … can you please come home?'

Ten minutes later he rushes through the front door, peeking into the living room to see if Tracy is there but finding Joey instead.

'Mammy is sad again, Daddy. Will you fix her?'

Giving his son a kiss and hug, Rob exits the living room and heads towards the kitchen, where Tracy is sitting at the table. She is crying, with her head nestled in her arms.

He sits beside her. 'Oh, love … Did you make an appointment with the doctor?'

'What's the point, Rob? He won't do anything. We've been here before. Why does it keep happening to us? What have we ever done wrong? I can't do this anymore, Rob – my heart is breaking, I can't handle it. I can't think straight anymore … it's just not right.'

'I'm going to call the doctor. I'll go with you, and we're not leaving until we get some answers.'

He gets an appointment straightaway.

Tracy straightens herself up, asks her mam to keep an eye on Joey, and leaves with Rob for the doctor's office. After a long wait, they are called in.

Rob explains. 'Doctor, Tracy has just lost again, and we want you to refer us as soon as possible for tests to find out what's wrong. It should not be this hard to have a baby. We have a healthy child already.'

'I am sorry to hear that news. I understand your frustr—'

'No, Doctor, please don't give us the spiel,' Rob interrupts. 'We just want a referral.'

'It's not that easy, Rob. At Tracy's age, it is not uncommon …'

'I don't want to hear that, Doctor. I'm sorry, but we are not leaving here without a referral.'

'Okay, I will refer you so that an investigation can take place …' He types on his computer keyboard, then hands a printout to Rob.

'Here, take this with you to the early pregnancy clinic today and they will get the ball rolling. That's all I can do. Tracy, do you need some tablets to help you cope with the stress?'

'No, thank you, Doctor. I just need some answers … like Rob said.'

'Very well. I will be in contact when I receive some results from the clinic.'

I considered the benefits of her encountering another gem and concluded that she received it because her profile states that she has a medical condition. I do not have the power to cure, but I do have the power to instigate action. I hope that by encountering yet another loss, Tracy will now be able to undergo an investigation. She will discover that she has a problem, and that will help her deal psychologically with the fact she was lucky to have received the miracle gift that is her young son, Joey. I have noted her desire to have a child. It is a pity that she was not the person who received the true gift, as she would have been an ideal candidate for the miracle that was released unknowingly …

CARRIE

I must move on now to Carrie. It looks as though she is getting ready to go to out. She is glowing with happiness, so I am holding out hope that maybe she has received the gift. I follow her and Tom to a family gathering, where they share their news with some of the family. They don't stay long, as they must ensure that they get their little Max home at a reasonable time. When they get back to the cottage, they all go to bed straightaway.

The next morning, Carrie is up first. She is a little concerned about something. When she comes out of the bathroom, she is as white as a sheet and rushes to the bedroom.

'Tom, there's something wrong.'

'Eh … err … what?' He tries to wake up so he can comprehend what she has just said.

'There's something wrong. There is some blood.' She is shaking.

He jumps out of bed and coaxes her back in. She lies there, afraid to move in case it might make matters worse.

'What can I do? Please tell me what I can do to help, Carrie.'

'I had better ring the doctor, so will you bring me my mobile?'

He goes out and comes back with her bag, setting it down gently beside her. They look lost; neither one knows what to do.

'Will you get Max some breakfast?'

'Sure thing. Can Iget you something? You will need to keep your strength up.'

'I really don't feel like anything … but I suppose you're right, I must … maybe a cup of tea and a piece of toast. Thanks.'

He leaves the room and she looks in her bag, trying to locate her mobile. She lifts out a card with a picture of an old woman on it. Carrie looks at it for a moment, then she kisses it and holds it close to her heart.

'Granny, if you can help, please don't let me lose this baby. Please, please, please.'

She starts to mumble, as if she is praying. Tears trickle from the sides of her closed eyelids. I will leave for now and call back later.

***

When I return, Carrie is still in bed. A woman who looks similar to her is sitting beside her on the bed. She gives her along, caring hug.

'Well, what did they say in hospital?'

'They said it is still there … but I might lose it, as I'm still bleeding.'

'How are you feeling?'

'A little confused and sad … I so want this baby, sis! I didn't know I did when I first found out, but I know now … I want another child so much. I just want the bleeding to stop.'

'Has it gotten any better?'

'No. It's worse. I know it is going to happen – it's just a matter of when.

'Oh, I am so sorry, Carrie! I feel so useless. I wish there was something I could do.'

'So do I, but all I can do is pray that it will all turn out wonderful in the end.'

I leave them as they hug again, as only sisters can.

***

When I return the following morning, I first assume that it was a sleepless night here. Carrie's eyes are red and she is no longer in bed. She is sitting in the living room and Tom sits beside her, holding her hand supportively.

Two older people are at the door; they knock and walk inside. I sense they are family. Maybe through Carrie's grief there has been a reunion of hearts.

'Hello, it's only us,' the woman calls out, walking over and giving Carrie a hug. 'So how are you feeling, love?'

'I'm not too bad, Mum, I just feel a little crappy, but I suppose I will for a while.'

'Don't worry, love … you will have another child.'

'I know, Mum, but that won't bring this one back, will it?'

Her father sits beside her on the sofa and puts his hand around her shoulder; it looks quite awkward, but she seems to have found a deep comfort from it.

'Don't worry, love … it will be fine in the end,' he says, and then he pulls her head onto his shoulder, as if she were his little girl again.

She closes her eyes for a moment as she drifts back to the sanctuary that was her father's embrace when she was a child. She has always loved her dad so much; he always protected her. She wants him to protect her from the pain and emptiness she is now feeling, and for those few moments he has done so.

The gem is doing its work here. For so long, Carrie has been filled with emptiness, unable to feel any emotion. Now she has the power to cry, the power to feel pain, and most importantly, the power to move on. She built a wall around herself for protection, without realising that, although it kept out sadness, it also kept out joy. It has been so long since she experienced any joy. That will all change now she has made the decision to move on.

But before I move on, I feel compelled to observe another interaction. This one is in a totally different setting; it seems to be a local playgroup. I see Carrie and Tracy standing beside each other as their two boys play trucks together.

'Yeah, he just proposed,' Carrie is saying. 'It was totally unexpected, but I was so happy; we've been through a bit of a rough time of it lately, but this has made the atmosphere in our home feel so much brighter.'

'Well, congratulations.'

'Thanks, Tracy.'

'A rough time … what happened?'

'Oh … we had a miscarriage, and I took it rather bad; but we are going to keep trying. He has been so strong for me.'

'I, too, recently had a miscarriage … it's tough.'

'Yeah, and people don't understand how hard it is unless they've had one themselves.'

'You're right, Carrie. Hey, do you fancy meeting up for a cuppa some day?'

'I'd love to.'

'What about tomorrow?' suggests Tracy. 'Our boys can have a play at my house, and I'll get some nice buns to make us feel better.'

'That sounds great. I'll look forward to it.'

How wonderful these two will be a great support for each other now – and their personalities complement each other, so they will make great friends.

Now I must move on, but I am so glad I stayed on to witness this.

BETHANY

I next visit Bethany to observe how she has progressed since experiencing the shock of the discovery that she is pregnant – followed so quickly by the shock of Hanson's proposal. She's had to absorb so many big changes in such a short time.

When I arrive at the apartment, paramedics rush past me, pushing a stretcher that holds an apparently unconscious and pale Bethany.

Across the stretcher, one paramedic shouts to the other, 'Tell ER to be ready. We'll be there in ten minutes!'

'What's going on? Is she going to be okay? Does this often happen after a miscarriage?' asks Hanson, panicked.

'I'm sorry, sir, but she's lost a lot of blood. Do you happen to know your fiancée's blood group?'

'No, sorry, I don't. But her mum should know.'

'Canyou call her? It's vitally important that we know. If her mum doesn't know, ask her for her own and Bethany's father's blood groups. We can work it out from there.'

Hanson calls from the ambulance on the way to thehospital but when he passes on the information, the paramedic shakes his head.

'She doesn't know for sure, but she thinks that Beth is AB-negative; her mum is O-positive, and her dad is A-positive.'

'She must have it wrong, because those blood groups would never match,' he says. 'We will have to conduct our own tests.'

'AB-negative is a rare blood group, so we may need her mother or father to donate blood because supplies are always low,' the other paramedic says. 'Will you call her mum back? Ask her or her husband – whichever one of them is also AB-negative – and tell them to get to the hospital ASAP. Their daughter's life depends on it.'

Struggling to remain calm, Hanson phones Beth's mum again. What she tells him causes the colour to drain from his face and after he hangs up he announces that Beth is definitely AB-negative, but her parents will be no help if she needs a transfusion.

I did not expect such a drama to be unfolding when I arrived. I will revisit later to see how things have developed.

***

When I arrive at the hospital the next morning, I am delighted to see Bethany sitting in bed, propped up by plump white pillows. Some colour has returned to her cheeks, but she is crying.

She speaks angrily to her mother. 'I was adopted? And you never told me? Did you never stop to think that I have a right to know – it does, after all, affect me. What right did you think you had – do you think you still have – to keep this information from me all of my life? Is it any wonder I never felt loved like a daughter should feel loved, or that I never felt a part of the family? I have always been your dress-up doll – a pretty plaything for you to showcase and get to win contests. That's all I ever was to you … all I ever will b—'

'No, Beth it wasn't like that. Your father and I have always loved you as much as we would have loved our own child.'

'What was it like, then? Please enlighten me.'

'I think you need to focus on getting better first, and then we will talk about it. You need some time to recover from your ordeal, and then you will be thinking more clearly.'

'Well, if you are not going to tell me anything, you may as well leave, because I really don't want you around me at the moment.'

'I understand, love … you know where I am if you need me.' Hil gets up and leaves the room.

Hanson stands up, sits beside Bethany on the bed and gives her a loving hug.

'Are you sure you still want to marry someone who doesn't even know who she is?'

'I am determined to marry you as soon as possible, especially if it will help you feel that you do have an identity.'

'Will you please promise me something, Han?'

'Of course … anything.'

'Promise me we will never lie to our children and that we will always be honest with each other – forever.'

He squeezes her tight and says, 'I promise I will never be untruthful to you or our children, Beth. I love you too much to hurt you.'

'I will also need some help finding my real parents, Han. Will you help me?'

'We will find them, Beth. Sure, you need your dad to walk you down the aisle.'

The gem has surely been hard at work here. Its departure has instigated realisations and revelations. Bethany has realised she does want children, after all; she is automatically seeing her future with children in it now. The revelation that she was adopted as a baby has been the biggest shock of all, but it seems to have provided her with the missing piece to the puzzle of her life – the piece she has always felt was missing. This would not have come to light if it had not been for the unfortunate event that was her need for urgent medical attention and blood. To top it off, the gem's arrival gave Hanson the opportunity to propose, which he had been waiting to do for some time. I believe a long and happy life together lies in store for this couple.

SIOBHAN

I will move on to Siobhan now. I feel as though she is calling me, and so I must answer. When I arrive, what I witness shocks me: the last time I saw her, she was quite rough and ready, as the shock of the real possibility of a child entering her life had begun to sink in. For the first time, I have not arrived at her workplace, which I find strange, as it is a midweek day.

Instead, I am at her home: a two-storey townhouse, not the type of property I would have visualised as Siobhan's residence. I go inside to discover she is not alone. Another woman must live there, too.

Siobhan has a different glow about her. Her aura is no longer an angry, fiery red, it has calmed down tremendously, and it is a little hazy, which indicates she is undergoing a personal transformation.

She has her hair down, but this time it looks healthy and shiny, and the red locks fall down over her shoulders. She is not wearing her military-style suit, either; a very flattering dress, bursting with colour, completes her bright new look.

She is making tea in the kitchen, and she carries a tray through to the back of the house, going outside to a high, raised deck section. Walking over to a table and chairs, she sets the tray on the table.

'Mum!' she calls. 'Tea is ready.'

'I'm coming, love,' her mum replies.

They both get comfortable, sitting with their feet up on the two spare chairs.

'This is really nice and peaceful, isn't it, Mum?'

'It's just perfect, love, and these eclairs are so yum.'

They sit in a contented silence for a few moments.

'So, Mr Maximus didn't mind your taking some leave, then?'

'No, he didn't, actually. I explained the situation, told him I was taking a year off, and he understood. He has decided to take Will on for that year. Will has great potential, as I had at his age, and it will be a great experience for him.'

'When is your scan, love?'

'I have one booked for next week. I'm so excited, Mum! Just look at me – to think that just a few months ago I was a very bitter person who felt nothing but frustration with others. Now, as I look back, I cringe at how I acted and how I treated people at work.'

'You weren't such a joy to be around at home, either, love. You were very cross – just like your dad was.'

'I know, and I am sorry, Mum. Things are going to be different now. I'm going to be a mum; and more importantly, I'm going to be a good mum.'

'You'll be a great mum, and I'll always be here to help.'

'I know, and I'm grateful for that. You know, I've been meaning to ask you something. Will you be the godmother? I think of you as the baby's guardian angel.'

Her mum smiles with delight. 'I would be honoured, love, and I promise that I will be a great godmother.'

'I've one more thing to tell you, Mum.'

'Oh, yes? What's that, love?'

'We're moving.'

This comes as a big surprise.

'Moving? Where are we moving? I hope it's not one of those high-rise apartment blocks. You know I wouldn't make it up the stairs if the lift was ever broken.'

'No, Mum, it's not an apartment. It's a bigger house on the outskirts of the city; it has green grass and a big backyard where this little one can play.' She pats her tummy affectionately. 'It's just perfect, Mum … you're going to love it. There's a flower garden for you to take care of, too.'

'Oh, love, it sounds absolutely perfect! I'll be ever so happy to spend time in a garden, filling the house with such beautiful colours and scents from the flowers I'll grow from seedlings.'

'It's going to be wonderful, Mum. This little gift has come to me at this time in my life for a reason: to change how I once was and to focus on the future, not just for myself but for all of us.'

'I'm so happy to hear that, love, because I felt so sad watching you self-destruct just like your dad did; he was his own worst enemy, you know. I have one thing to ask you – and I hope you don't mind my being so direct – but, who is the baby's father?'

'Let's just say that he is in the know, but he chooses not to be part of it, as he is focusing on forwarding his own career right now.'

Wow – what a shocker! Her life now has purpose and meaning. I must admit that when I first realised a gift had been released, Siobhan was the one person I hoped would not receive it. I judged her by the way she treated others, and I realise that by doing so, I was as judgemental as she was. It hurts to admit that, but I must, because it is true. I should have realised her aggressive behaviour had to stem from a missing link in her life. Now, after what I have just observed, I am comfortable and happy knowing that Siobhan is carrying my gift. She is strong in mind, and she knows what she wants for her child. The support she will receive from her mum's warm and caring nature will help the child grow up with strong foundations for a good life. That's the best we can ever hope to give our children.

I am getting all emotional, and I feel connected to Siobhan and her mum. I suppose that is because I know it is my gift which Siobhan has received. Nevertheless, my observations here are complete, and I cannot wait to share my discovery with Syd. I know she will be so pleased for me.

Chapter Fifteen
The Final Observation

This now means that Kath has also received a gem, so it will be interesting to observe how she is progressing on her journey of transition. As soon as I arrive at the location, I home in on her essence. She is back in hospital again, but James is with her. It seems they are spending a lot of time together, so at least she is not alone. Isolation at a time of personal trauma can lead to internal combustion, as we feel the emotions more intensely when we have no-one to share them with. Hence, the saying: 'A problem shared is a problem halved.'

'Why are we never to share a child, James?' Kath says. 'Is this some type of sign to let us know that we should not be together?'

'Oh, Kath, please don't think like that! The whole ordeal has brought us closer together; I feel more determined to make things work for us, and I hope that you do, too.'

'You're right there. My first reaction when I found out we were expecting was, "Oh, no, not again … this man must have super sperm!" but that was only because it wasn't exactly how I had planned it would happen.'

'Let's look at it like this, then: now we have the opportunity to plan it.'

'James, I so want us tohave a child together … maybe it will be third time lucky. What do you reckon?'

'I love you, Kath. I missed you so much when we were forcibly separated all those years ago, even though we were only children. But that's just it: we were children. We didn't have a say, and we couldn't have made a go of it on our own. Now, all these years later, we can! I want us to really make a go of things. I know that this is a sad time for us – it is hard to lose a pregnancy, let's not let it be in vain. We are in control here, and we can turn this negative into a positive. I want to spend the rest of my life with you, Kath. Will you marry me?'

'Are you serious?'

'I have never been more serious about anything in my life. You are the woman for me, and I don't want to lose you again.'

'Yes, James, I will marry you.'

They hug and kiss – a long, passionate and loving kiss.

'When are you going to be allowed to get out of here?'

'I'm not sure yet, but I can't see any reason why they might want me to stay. It's not like they can do very much for me now … Why do you ask?'

'Well, we have a ring to buy.'

'Oh, right … I'll call the nurse.'

They smile at each other.

I will leave them now. Well, what a turn-up for the books this is! The gem has certainly moved things along nicely, here. It seems that these two are supposed to be together, through destiny – maybe as teenagers they met too soon. The gem has given them the opportunity to get close enough emotionally to realise theycan trust each other.

My final observation is now complete, so it is time to return to the Waiting Zone. However, I find myself drawn back to Kath's house, although I don't know why. I have finished all the observations, which means my assignment is complete; still, I sense that it is not time to leave yet, as I have something more to witness.

I allow the energy to draw me, and a short time later, I arrive at Kath's house. Kath and James enter the house and she is carrying a little bag that has what looks like a ring box in it. They rush into the living room.

'Let me do this right, Kath.' Taking the bag from her grasp, James gets down on one knee.

'What are you doing, James? Don't be silly!' she says, giggling with delight.

'I can't have you saying that I didn't do this properly, now, can I?'

He takes the box from the bag and opens it, revealing a dazzling diamond ring.

'Katherine Johnston, will you do me the honour of becoming my wife?'

'James Justin Joyce, it would be my absolute pleasure – and it's about time, too, I must add.'

He stands up, pulls her up into his arms, lifts her off her feet and swings her around.

The telephone rings, and she says, 'I had probably better get that.'

'Ah, do you have to?'

'Yes, it might be important.'

She doesn't make it in time. It rings off and the answering

machine starts. Kath's recorded voice fills the room: 'Hello,you have reached the messaging bank for Kath Johnston. Please leave a message after the beep.'

'Oh, don't you just hate hearing your own voice on those bloody machines? It is just so embarrassing!' says Kath as a flush glows on her cheeks.

A man's voice leaves a message: 'Hello, Kath Johnston. You probably won't know me, but my name is Hanson Jones, and I am the fiancé of Bethany Moore. I don't know if you know Beth, but she is a model. Anyway, that has nothing to do with why I have called … it's a little awkward, you see … I won't say it on a machine, so could you call me as soon as you can? My number is—'

In the meantime, Kath has run to the telephone, and she picks up the handset, interrupting Hanson's message.

'Hello, Hanson. This is Kath, here; you don't need to leave a message … Yes, that is correct … Is this for real? You are not joking me …? Yes, of course I do … Will you tell her that I will have someone else for her to meet also …? Yes, thank you for calling, Hanson, I will be indebted to you for the rest of my life …'

She hangs up the phone, laughing and crying at the same time, and she starts dancing around the room, unable to hide her excitement.

'Are you going to ever tell me just what is going on?' James asks.

Kath stops dancing. In-between her tears and laughter, she begins to explain the message to James.

'Do you know Hanson Jones? He's an actor.'

'Yes, I think so. Why?'

'Well, he's about to become your son-in-law.'

'What are you talking about, woman? Have you gone completely mad? Did they give you too many painkillers in the hospital?'

'No, silly! It's all come back to us, James, can't you see? We have trusted our love for each other, and it has turned full circle to bring us magnificent joy. The call was about our daughter – the one who was taken away from us. She never knew she was adopted until recently. She had a miscarriage, needed a blood transfusion and the truth came out. Her fiancé retraced records and found a link with the name Katherine Johnston, so he has been ringing all the Katherine Johnstons he could find. Luckily, he found me – I mean us! Do you understand what I'm telling you, James? We have got our little girl back; she was lost, and now she is found – my lovely little princess who was stolen from my body in the harshest way imaginable has come back to me! Now I can be a proper mum for her at a time when she needs a mum to love her, and when I need a child to love. Thank you, whatever divine intervention has made this happen! Thank you, from the bottom of my heart.'

James drops onto the chair, speechless, as he allows it all to sink in.

'Oh, and by the way, she's getting married next month, so you may get the tux out – she will probably need you to give her away … James, are you okay?'

'Just nip me, Kath. I have to be dreaming … How can one day go from being complete and utter devastation to complete and utter joy so quickly? I'm going to need time to let it sink in.'

'You don't have time for it to sink in, James. Come on … we're going out.'

'Where are we going?'

'We're going to meet her.'

'What … already? Can't it wait until we're ready?'

'Wait? Are you kidding me? I have waited twenty-two years to hold her in my arms – do you think I'm going to wait one minute longer? Are you coming?'

'Yes, of course I am.'

Grabbing their coats, he follows her out the door.

My work here is done; they have finally found each other. It is amazing how, when something in life is destined for you, it won't pass you by twice. It may take a while if it misses you the first time, but it will always come back – and when it does, it will be even bigger and better than the first time.

Chapter Sixteen

Back in the Zone

I can't wait to catch up with Syd! She will be so interested in finding out who I believe should receive the gift, as she is a real believer in children being born to parents who will love and protect them as much as possible. This belief stems from Syd witnessing bad parenting when she was young. She has often recounted to me the horror that was her childhood, and as a result of her experience, she understands the detrimental impact this can have on children and their life foundations. I so appreciate Syd's values, especially when it comes to the final decision at the team meeting.

The gift of life is the most precious gift of all, and it should never be given to those who don't appreciate it, as they will only pass those negative values on to their children, who will then pass them onto their children, and so on – and the knock-on effect is drastic. That is why, here in the Waiting Zone, we try our best to eliminate the possibility of that happening. When we do our jobs well, we are able to control some of the reciprocators of the gift of life.

I go straight to Syd's quarters. She does not answer, so I ring again. No, she is definitely not there. I was supposed to be back sooner, but I got so caught up in things that I didn't even think of messaging Syd to let her know I would be delayed. Oh, goodness! I know all too well how she always thinks of the worst-case scenario.

How inconsiderate am I? I will have to make it up to her somehow. I had better contact her now and hope that she will meet me. I send her a message: *Syd, I am back. Can we meet? Sorry I didn't message sooner! Roo.*

I head back to my own quarters to wait for Syd to respond. Time passes, but still there is no reply. It is not like her to give the cold shoulder for long – she likes to get things sorted out straightaway. As I leave my quarters, I cross the corridor to ring her bell again; still no reply. I resend the message and I hear a receptor beeping in her flat; either she is there and not letting me in, or she has gone out and forgot to take her message connector.

I decide to go in search of her, as that is the only way I will find out what is going on. The first person I bump into along the way is Jonnie.

'Ah, Jonnie … thank goodness! How are you?'

'I'm good, mate. How did your assignment go?'

'Interestingly. Have you seen Syd around?'

'Not since this morning. Gee, she hasn't been the same since she got back from meeting you. What did you do to her, Roo? I could hardly talk to her without her biting my head off for no reason whatsoever.'

'I didn't do anything, Jonnie. We had a great time together.'

'Would it have anything to do with you leaving us, do you think?'

'Erm … I haven't really considered how Syd feels about my leaving. Thanks for the wake-up call, buddy.'

'You're welcome, mate! Don't forget – meeting tomorrow morning. Nine o'clock!' Jonnie shouts after me, as I have already turned around, quickly moving along the corridor back to Syd's quarters.

Ah, Syd! How selfish am I? I'm some friend. When I arrive back at her door, I knock continuously.

'Open up, Syd! I know you're in there, and I am not leaving until you talk to me! I mean it, Syd – I can do this all night, but then we will just be wasting more time—'

The door unlocks and I let myself in. Syd doesn't look happy, and her eyes are bloodshot, which means that either she was on the alcopops again, or she has been crying. I presume the latter.

'Syd, I am so going to miss you. Thirty-four years …'

'Please don't, Roo; I just need some time alone. I always knew you would go before me, but I can't believe it's happening right now.'

'You know that I will be waiting for you, and your time will be along soon, too … just you wait and see.'

'What am I supposed to do until then, Roo? I don't think I can bear being hooked up with a new partner. Did you hear that Jayden is supposed to be the one allocated as Visitor once you're gone?'

'You have to be kidding me! Boss can't do that; sure, wasn't it Jayden who sabotaged the gems in the first place? But hey, let's not get into all that now.'

'When are you scheduled to leave?'

'As far as I know, it's set for the day after tomorrow.'

'I must focus. I have to get a grip; enough of this feeling sorry for myself. My best friend is about to go forth to once again hold the woman he loves in his arms; and this time, it will be for all eternity. So I must give him a send-off to remember.'

'Ah, Syd, please … really, you don't have to do that. I just want to spend as much time as possible with you before I leave.'

'And you will, because you can help me organise it.'

'Oh, okay. And I suppose I don't have a say in this, do I?'

'No.'

'Are you sure we were never married, Syd?'

'Ha-ha! You would be so lucky. Anyway, I have decided that you are right now going to pop down to Dave's to get an obscene amount of Heavenly delights, while I put together two fluffy-dream large espressos, and then we are going to sit down for the rest of the evening and have a laugh and a giggle like we always do. Then you will fill me in on everything that happened in the final observation. How does that sound to you?'

'As always, Syd, that sounds perfect. You have read my mind, as usual.'

'That's just one of my many talents, you know.'

'Oh, yes, I know that … don't you worry.'

I leave for Dave's, and return carrying a whole tray of delights. I am sure that anyone who saw me on my way back must have wondered what I was doing with so many, but these cakes are just so good – and, oh boy, am I going to miss them when I leave. I wonder if they deliver to Heaven …

I spend the whole evening at Syd's. We sit, snuggled on the cosy couch, reminiscing about all the things we've done together over the years. We laugh and relax all evening – and well into the early hours of the morning, when, at some point, we fall asleep in each other's arms. I wake at seven thirty, which is very late, as I have a lot of organising to complete before the meeting at nine o'clock. I slip out of Syd's grasp, stretching my body as I am rather stiff after being in that cramped position for some time.

I take a moment to look at Syd before I leave. She lies in peaceful beauty on the couch, her golden locks spread out everywhere.

'You are beautiful, and I am going to miss you so much,' I whisper, bending down and kissing her tenderly on the forehead.

Turning away abruptly, I leave her quarters.

Chapter Seventeen

Final Meeting

As I approach the boardroom, I sense a change in the atmosphere. No-one is standing outside the door in a military fashion. They are all already in the boardroom, sitting comfortably in the fluffy white chairs that just swallow you up as though they were clouds or marshmallows, not chairs at all. Everyone seems to be in a good mood, chatting and laughing and joking with one another.

I enter, and although they must struggle to get out of the chairs, eventually, they all stand up and clap as I take my seat. I am kind of embarrassed but also honoured.

The Boss enters the room. Everyone is quiet once again; I am in awe of his sense of presence, which I could never equal.

'Good morning, everyone.'

'Good morning, Boss.'

'As everyone has probably heard by now, a long-standing member of the team has earned his right to enter the gates of Heaven. Congratulations, Rupert.'

Everyone starts to clap.

'Well done, Rupert!' a few of the guys shout.

Boss continues, 'So, Rupert, we would like to say that we wish you all the best for your eternity – may it be all that you have ever wanted it to be.'

'Thanks, Boss.'

'However, we must put that aside for the moment and focus on the job in hand. You have had a busy time on this assignment. Please fill us all in now, so that we will be able reach our final decisions as to who we consider worthy of receiving the gifts.'

I take a quick glance at Syd, who is looking at me in a strange but caring way.

'Yes, of course, Boss. I will start with Carrie. When I first started observing, she was in a disturbing state. She was living day by day, just trying to survive. The relationship between her and her partner was deteriorating rapidly, as he tried to get an emotional reaction from her by being mean and she just deflected it; this was so destructive for their relationship. I had to release a crystal just to get them close enough to have the opportunity to release the gem.

'I completed an energy check on their home, only to discover a hostile energy field. He was not happy that they were not married – and not even thinking of marriage – and so he continuously projected negative energies throughout the house. I tried to cleanse the home, but the negativity was just so strongly rooted that I couldn't shift it. When the gem was released and the discovery was made, it brought Carrie and Tom together; they believed their bad luck had changed. She took the loss very badly, and she realised just how much she wanted another child. She also recognised how supportive her partner had been throughout the experience, and so, when he proposed, she said yes.

'They are now able to deflect any negative energies. Plus, because they will soon be married, the negative energy force should stop his release, and their luck will now change for the better. I believe the gem has done its work here, and that this couple are ready to have another child.'

'Right. Very good … so who's next?'

'Yes, next …' (I rustle through the file; I never remember the order of my observations.) 'That would be … Tracy. When I first observed Tracy, I noticed that a very sombre energy was always present everywhere around her. Everything seemed so dull and negative. The past losses affected her badly, and she feels the mental and emotional strain. All she can think about is the past; she can't focus on the future, or even the present.

'She has always had a lot of losses to deal with: her father passed on when she was young, and he has been a spirit in the house ever since – in fact, he is the one projecting the dull, negative energy force. I explained to him how he could move on, and as soon as he did so, the energy flow changed colour immediately – it was amazing how much brighter things seemed … instantly.

'Anyway, during the flashbacks, I learned about a past loss, and I was also brought back a few years prior to a happier time for her, when she was planning to elope with her then-fiancé, who is now her husband, Rob. Because of this gem, I believe she will get some medical answers as to why she is having so many issues keeping a pregnancy – her profile indicates a medical condition. These answers will help her to move forward and deal with her emotions, so that she can appreciate what she has and not focus on what she doesn't have.

'In the words of Oprah Winfrey, "Be thankful for what you have; you'll end up having more. If you concentrate on what you don't have, you will never ever have enough." I don't believe that we can intervene when it is a medical issue, and I have wondered why a gem was sent to her again, but it is clear she needs closure. She needs a medical professional to spell it out for her, letting her know how lucky she has been to have had her first child. This final gem has given the push, enabling that to happen, when up to now, she had lost all hope.'

'Interesting observation, Rupert … go on, please,' says Boss.

'Next was Bethany – such a young thing … only twenty-two, but so in love with her partner. She has had a tough life, as her mum pushed her so hard to be successful in a modelling career that she didn't have a childhood at all. During the flashbacks, I witnessed just how intense this pressure was, and how her mum pushed her dad away from the situation.

'Beth and her fiancé are perfect for each other; he just worships her, and she feels so lucky to have his unconditional love and support. At first, she thought she did not want to have a baby, but I believe that was only because of her own mother's behaviour. As time and events progressed – and especially after she discovered her partner's desire to settle down and have children, not to mention his surprise proposal – her perspective on her surprise pregnancy changed.

'However, when the gem returned, complications resulted; she needed blood, which led to her discovering that her parents were not her birth parents – she had been adopted as an infant, but never knew. This freed her from the shackles of blind loyalty to her mother, whom Beth never felt really loved her as a daughter.

'Things have dramatically progressed, as it turns out that Beth is linked to Kath, who is the next recipient of the gem that I have to report on.

'Kath had a horrific teen experience: when she was fifteen, she fell for a cocky lad called James. She ended up pregnant, and her parents sent her to a convent where she endured six months of sadness, only for it to end in horror as her child was snatched from her as soon as she was born. Kath never married, but she did become very successful in the fitness field. She attended a school reunion, where she and James saw each other again for the first time since the trauma. They hit it off straightaway, and he was the instigator of the release of the gem. The news of her expecting drew them together.

'When the gem left her body, she was devastated, but he helped her though it … and even proposed! That same day, Bethany's fiancé tracked Kath down to let her know that she is Bethany's birth mum – which also means that James is her biological dad – and so they all arranged to meet. The gem's main purpose was actually to reunite these two women, as their opportunity for a lifetime of happiness together was stolen from them. Those who take it upon themselves to play God with others' lives should have consequences to pay themselves. Mind you, Kath's father lost the love of his daughter because of his actions; at least Kath now has the chance to redeem her love for her child.

'They both can now move on to the next stages of their lives together, and it is my opinion that they are both ideal candidates to receive a gift. And why not make it a fairytale come true? Let them share their pregnancies together, as there would be no stronger way for them to seal their bond.'

'That is a Hollywood blockbuster all in itself, Rupert. It fairly pulls at the heartstrings,' Boss says. 'Who was last?'

'Yes, that was Siobhan. After first observing her, I was so shocked that she was even considered for receipt of a gem, never mind a gift. I was shown a seductive young woman with no moral standards, who would do anything at all to get what she wanted. She was ruthless when it came to talking to others, showing no regard or consideration for their feelings whatsoever. Her tongue was like a lightning bolt, firing insults with no hesitation, showing no concept of consequence. It was all very disturbing to watch.

'I went back to her childhood, only to discover that her father was a brutally harsh man, humiliating both her and her mother at any opportunity. It was plain to see that her mother was a broken woman, but I never got to see her face, as her head was always down, and her hair covered any part of her face that might have been visible. The poor woman must have had no self-confidence left! This man was the energy vampire, and she was his victim.

'Siobhan surprised me on the final observation, however; when I arrived, I discovered that she had made a total transformation from a vixen to a woman of substance. I was shocked to discover that she was the recipient of my gift, and even with my discovery of her metamorphosis, an initial horror overcame my thoughts. But, I soon realised that it was the best thing that had ever happened to her, and it has now transformed her into an ideal candidate for a gift.'

'So, considering all these facts, Rupert, which three women would you like us to vote for?' asks Boss.

'Siobhan has already received a gift, so she is no longer in the running. Of the four women left, I wish I could send each of them a gift, but as only three gifts are available, I would send the first gift to Carrie, as she is so ready. I would send the second gift to Bethany, and the third to Kath. I would love to send a gift to Tracy, and initially I hoped that she had received the miracle that was the release of my gift; but on further consideration, I believe that she is not yet ready, as she needs to get the medical investigation out of the way first.'

'Thank you for your detailed analysis, Rupert,' Boss says. Turning to the group, he instructs, 'In light of what you all have just heard, I want you to write down your nominations. When you are finished, send them to the top table for counting.'

This process takes about twenty minutes, which I suppose is not bad, really … but it is rather boring.

At last, Boss announces, 'The nominations have been counted, and I can now tell you who will receive a gift, and in what order: Bethany will be the first to receive a gift, Kath will be second and Carrie will be third. I am sure we all hope that someday Tracy will be in a position to receive a gift.'

Everyone agrees.

'Now that all of the formalities are out of the way, as Rupert is leaving us tomorrow, we can't let him go without a bit of a send-off.'

Boss turns toward the boardroom door.

The door opens, and a giant Heavenly delight cake is wheeled in. I can't believe my eyes, and my poor stomachis screaming 'no more', as I overdosed on the sugary delights last night at Syd's.

Everyone cheers as Boss says, 'Let the party begin!'

Chapter Eighteen

Entering the Gates

So it is finally here. The day I have been waiting on for thirty-four years has finally arrived. The day has come when I finally get to hold my dearly beloved Josie in my arms again. The gates of Heaven will open wide for me today as I receive the right to enter. I have finally been forgiven for the sin I made all those years ago. I have earned eternal happiness, and the feeling is overwhelming.

Mind you, the feeling of nausea is quite overwhelming, too, as I really did overdo it on the Heavenly delights last night. The party was great, and it was such a wonderful 'surprise'. Syd really went out of her way to make my last night in the Waiting Zone a memorable one. I had the opportunity to hang with everyone I have come to know over the time I have been here, and I value that so much. I am almost sad to leave, as this has been my 'little Heaven' for so long.

I must start getting ready for dispatch; although I do not need to take anything with me, I have still to mentally prepare myself to leave, as my desire is not to leave. Of course, I want eternal happiness with Josie and our child, but I also love the zone and all my friends here – especially Syd. The only thingI will bring with me is a gift from Syd – it is a gold chain and pendant that she gave me last night when we said our final goodbye. The pendant bears two engravings: *Special Friend* on the front, and on the back, *Your memory is engraved in my heart forever – Syd.* She wouldn't let me open it last night while she was there, but when I got back to my quarters and opened it, I just sat and stared. It sums it all up: I now realise that she has strong feelings for me, but I am not in the position to consider my feelings for her – other than the deep feeling of friendship – and so I don't.

It is time for me to make my way to dispatch. I exit my quarters and close the door, turning around to see Syd's door. I stare at it for a moment; the desire to knock on it and embrace her is overwhelming … but I can't do that, so I shake that thought right out of my head.

I start walking down the corridor. Just as I reach the stairs, I hear a voice call from behind me.

'Roo! Hold on a moment.'

I turn around to see Syd running as fast as she can down the corridor. She is wearing her polka-dot pyjamas and her cow slippers that moo when you squeeze the toes. I laugh and my heart warms at this vision of utter silliness.

When she finally reaches me, she says defensively, 'What are you laughing at? Here I am, making an effort to say goodbye, and all you can do is laugh!'

'Oh, Syd, just be quiet.'

Pulling her towards me, I give her the strongest, warmest, most caring hug that I have ever given anyone. She stays there, so content to be in my arms.

'I am going to miss you so much, Syd ... I can only hope that it won't be long before you finally join me.'

'Roo, it is too long already.' She pushes herself away from me and holds onto my lapel. 'And anyway, you're finally going to be reunited with the love of your life. You've waited for this day for a lifetime, so I will not hold you back – I just wanted to say that I hope it all goes as you have dreamt it would for as long as I've known you.'

'Thanks, Syd. I'm going to miss you so much ... I had better go.'

I do something now that is the hardest thing I have ever had to do. Ever. I turn around and walk away; my stomach wrenches.

I arrive in dispatch, and who is the first person I bump into? Jayden – of course!

'Well, well, Rupert. You are finally moving on.'

'Hello, Jayden. I thought you no longer worked here.'

'It is my last day,' he beams proudly. 'Have you any advice for me, seeing as I will be slipping into your shoes? Maybe you can fill me in on how to get close to Syd ...'

Enraged, I make a go for him; Jonnie, who happens to arrive just in time, is the only thing that saves Jayden.

'Don't you listen to him, Roo, he's just trying to rise you ... I will be taking care of Syd when you go, so don't worry about him.'

I give Jayden a stare that speaks volumes, and he smugly smirks back. Oh, he does rise me; it kills me that he is going to be the person who takes over my job as Visitor –he has no values and so much to learn.

'So, Roo, I am gonna miss you, mate!' Jonnie says. 'The place isn't gonna be the same without you.'

'Thanks for saying that Jonnie ... and for coming to see me off.'

'What are mates for?'

'You will keep an eye on Syd for me, won't you?'

'I promise I will. Listen, I better get back, mate. I wish you all the best … you never know, I might see you in Heaven someday.'

We give each other a man hug and I set off down the long corridor to the dispatch lounge.

Harry, ever his calm self, is on duty again. I have yet to meet a person as relaxed about life as he is. It is a calming experience just to interact with him.

'Hello, Rupert. You back again so soon?'

'Yeah, Harry. I'm on my final journey to the gates of Heaven.'

'Well, good for you, buddy! I'm so glad for you … you've waited a long time for this to come along.'

'You're right, there, Harry.'

'What's up? You don't seem to be as chuffed as I would have expected you to be.'

'Oh, it's nothing. It's just … ah, I'm being silly. I'm just a bit nervous, is all. To wait so long for something to come … and then, when it does finally happen, it's a bit surreal, and I don't know what to expect.'

'It will be whatever you think it to be, Rupert. You have the power to control your thoughts: if you want it to be wonderful, it will be – but if you have already decided that it is not, it won't be. The mind is a powerful device, you know.'

'Oh, I know Harry; you seem to have it sussed, though. What's your secret?'

'Now that would be telling, wouldn't it?'

We go through the usual protocol before I reach the Vortex. As I stand there, ready to dispatch for the last time, I have an overwhelming feeling of nervous excitement at the prospect of my reunion with Josie – and I start to wonder if things could ever be as they once were. Have I been unrealistic about the situation and romanticised it to be more than it ever possibly could be? I will never know unless I go and find out. So I give the thumbs up to Harry and enter the Vortex.

When travelling in the Vortex, I am more aware of myself and my past, which the Vortex picks up on. As a result, snapshots from my memory start to flash around me. It is all quite startling, to be honest, as I see images of Josie as she was on our honeymoon, laughing and happy; and then I see images of her in hospital, followed by images of me jumping off the bridge. Finally, I see images of Syd and some of the things we did together. The whole journey through the Vortex consisted of what I can only describe as a movie of my life up to now.

It certainly has been an eye-opener. When I finally arrive at the gates of Heaven, I need to take a few moments to compose myself.

Wow! I have always known it would be a spectacular entrance, and I am not disappointed. Even so, I could never have imagined such magnificence. God must really know what He wants when it comes to making a statement. The gates, constructed of the richest gold I have ever seen, rise higher than I can view. A constant gleam shines from them, projecting angelic rays everywhere. It is utterly mesmerising, and I can see why people passing on from Earth are drawn towards the light; it must act as a beacon, guiding them to Paradise.

I check that I have my pass ready, as I am next in the queue to enter. I see what I can only describe as a Heavenly ticket box, and I watch as the people ahead of me hand their passes in and receive stamps on their hand as if they were about to enter a concert. It is my turn, and I submit my pass and receive the stamp, which doesn't dye my hand … it sort of glows there like a tiny neon sign. It's very strange. As I follow the queue towards the gates, I get the first view of people waiting for their loved ones to enter. The feeling among the crowd is one of mixed emotions – anticipation, nervousness, excitement at the prospect of reunion with lost loved ones; yet, on the other hand, sadness for the ones they have left behind. I, too, feel this way, even though I have come from a different place. These similar feelings unite us all.

I look for the familiar beautiful face that stole my heart all those years ago, scan the crowds for her auburn hair that swept down over her shoulders. I am almost at the gates, but I still have had no glimpse of her.

The gateman, sensing my anticipation, comments, 'Have you not spotted anyone waiting yet?'

To which I reply, 'No. I expected my wife to be waiting with our child, but I cannot see her yet.'

'Well, just you keep to the left at all times, do you hear? That is the way to your eternal destiny.'

'Oh … okay … thanks.'

It doesn't make any sense to me, but I take it onboard, as you never know what information may come in handy.

I enter through the gates to see a place of divine beauty. It is everything I have ever imagined … and more; it even outshines any picture that I have ever created in my colourful, imaginative mind. I am awestruck, gobsmacked with utter amazement. I stand still, while people rush past me into the arms of their loved ones. I snap out of my daydream. Once again, I scan the crowd, peering at everyone in view, straining to find what I have always imagined this moment would be: Josie waiting for me, holding our baby in her arms; as she catches sight of me, she runs into my arms, longing for my warm embrace … and she clings to me, never wanting me to let her go, ever again. This is what I have imagined for the past thirty-four years, but she is nowhere in sight … no sign of her at all. I have a strange feeling that something isn't right. This is not supposed to be the way it ends for me – I just know it …

Someone taps me on the back, and my heart skips a beat. I turn around, only to discover Tracy's father standing there, with Tracy's mother at his side.

'Thank you for helping me to pass on, young man,' hesays.

'You are very welcome.'

'This is my wife, and we are finally together again.'

'Hello, nice to meet you,' I say.

'Nice to meet you, too,' she replies.

'We had better be off now … you take care.'

'Thank you … I will.'

I suddenly realise that, as Tracy's mother has passed on, she will now have the power to send Tracy a miracle gift, so I call out to them.

'Sorry! Hold on a moment … I must let you know that you can send your gift to Tracy to enable her to have the second child she has always wanted.'

'Really? I would so love to be able to do that!' her mother says. 'The poor love has been devastated by the news that she is not capable of carrying another child, and if I can send her one … oh, it would mean so much. Thank you for taking the time to tell me, son.'

'You're welcome … I wish you both eternal happiness.' They smile and walk on.

I look around, but I do not have a clue which way to go. Two signs point to different paths. One sign says *Eternal Happiness* and points to the path on the right. I so want to walk down this path, but I feel compelled to check out the other sign; first, because the gateman said to 'stay to the path on the left', but also because I don't want to head down the path to eternal happiness without Josie and our child. The other sign says *The Waiting Zone.* Now I am really confused! I have just come from the Waiting Zone, but I reason that this must be a sort of waiting room that coincidentally has the same name. I start to walk along the path towards reception.

Who is the first person I meet? None other than Boss.

'I don't mean to be rude, Boss, but I thought I would not be seeing you for a while.'

'Rupert, I am glad you found your way. You got the directions okay from the gateman, then.'

'Yeah, I suppose. What's going on, Boss? My head is spinning. I need some answers.'

'Alright, you have been through enough, Rupert. I have those answers for you.'

'Great! Why am I back here with you, then? Please tell me that.'

'I'm glad you have asked me that first. Please follow me to the office.'

Once there, we both take a seat – not at opposite sides of his desk, though; we sit on the sofa in the corner of his office, as if we are about to have a sociable chat.

'Now, Rupert, I must ask you to be prepared for a shock, as what I am going to tell you will be… unexpected.'

'I'm tougher than you think, Boss, and anything you say cannot be worse than the thoughts that are entering my head right now.'

'Josie is not here to meet you.'

'What? Why?'

'She did not die. She had complications, but she did not die – you did not hang around long enough to find out what happened.'

'What about the baby? Where is the baby?'

'The baby survived, too.S he also had complications, but they stuck together and got through it.'

'I'm sorry … I don't understand. Why did I not know this before now? Why have I been in the Waiting Zone all this time, living in the hope of being reunited with them, thinking they were here all along, just waiting on me … when they weren't. You must have known, Boss, you should have told me.'

'It was not my place to tell you, Rupert. They are living their life on Earth as they are meant to. I can't control that, but I can influence it slightly.'

'What do you mean?'

'I suppose I have to tell you.' Boss pauses. 'Rupert, this is going to put your life in a whole different perspective, I must warn you of that. Now you must think about this carefully. Do you want me to tell you something that will change you forever?'

'I must know, Boss! I've been living a lie for long enough – what I must have done to my poor Josie! She needed me, and I just left her on her own with our child. I had the one thing I have always wanted, and I threw it away in a moment of insanity. Why did I not just stay with them? They needed me – why did I not stay?'

'You must try to control your thoughts, Rupert; they will run wild if you don't try to control them. There is nothing you can change about it now. Things have moved on, and you must deal with these new revelations when your body tells you that it is ready.'

'You're right, of course, Boss. No need to panic; all will be well. Please go on.'

'You have met them since.'

This I cannot comprehend.

'Siobhan is your daughter, Rupert. That is why I arranged for her to receive your gift, as she was taking the wrong path, mowing people over as she sped along the road of life, caring only about herself and achieving power. She had so much hatred inside her; but when your gift entered her body, it was as though you gave her some part of you that she had not received at birth. Suddenly, she began to see things more positively … she began to value life and care about people.'

'Siobhan? But I saw her … I watched as she … excuse me, Boss.'

I run to the private toilet in Boss' office, where I vomit uncontrollably. The flashbacks of some of the seedy acts I witnessed her perform flood through my mind; it was such a gut-wrenching thing to discover that Siobhan is my daughter. I always knew she was some father's daughter, but I thought Mike was her father, and she'd turned out the way she did because of that … That bastard! What he did to my daughter! I need to be sick again. I should have been there for her … I clean myself up quickly, as I must get back out to the Boss.

'Now let me get this straight, Boss: Siobhan is my daughter, but what about Rosie? Who is she?'

'Rosie is Josie, Rupert. She was never the same after her illness, and then when she discovered that you had … well … you know … let's just say that she didn't deal with it very well. Her unwavering belief and faith was never the same. She ended up marrying Mike Roe in an attempt to get a father figure for Siobhan. She very rarely showed her face, as she lost a lot of her confidence, and that is why you didn't recognise her. She also changed her name to Rosie, because Mike didn't like the name Josie. I can understand how you wouldn't have guessed. But, as you can see now, Josie and Siobhan are very happy, and it is because of the gift you have sent them. Their lives have turned around for the better, and your gift will bring them so much joy … for the rest of eternity.'

'Yes … and I can wait here for them until then.'

'Well, it is not as simple as that, Rupert. They have now lived thirty-four years without you: Siobhan doesn't even know who you are; Josie will find love again, and she will be very happy – and he is the one who will wait for her at the gates of Heaven. It is entirely your decision, but I am offering you the opportunity to take a chance and wait here – or to return to the Waiting Zone.'

'Whoa! Back to the Waiting Zone? I never thought I would be doing that!'

'Listen, Rupert, I have something else to share with you.'

'I don't know if I can take any more, Boss.'

'I must confess that I have not been fully straight up with you. The fact that your gift was released was not a mistake or a sabotage mission planned by Jayden; I ordered him to do it, and I told him to be quiet about it.'

'What? But, why, Boss?'

'I am sorry, Rupert, but if you're going to keep interrupting, I won't get to tell you everything.'

'Oh, right … okay …sorry.'

'I have been the Boss of the Waiting Zone for more years than I care to remember. It so happens that I would like to move on now. I would finally like to take the path to eternal happiness. My wife is due to pass on shortly, and I would like to be the one who meets her at the gate.'

'With all due respect, Boss, can I ask what this has to do with me?'

'Rupert, I would like you to become the Boss of the Waiting Zone. I have watched you for many years, as I always knew that I would need a successor someday. And you are the ideal candidate.'

'Me – Boss of the Waiting Zone?'

'Yes, why not? You will then have full control of your own destiny. If it doesn't work out, you can do what I am doing: allocate someone else to take your place, and then you can enter Heaven again, as you have earned the right to do. It is your call, Rupert. I will leave it with you, as you have a lot to absorb at once.'

'It is a lot for me to take in, Boss, you sure are right, there. Can I be quite honest with you? I am rather relieved by this turn of events, as I think this may end up being the best outcome for me. Can I go back to the zone straight away?'

'Yes, of course, Rupert. But before you do, I just want to share a few words of advice, if I may.'

'Yeah, please do, Boss! I'm in need of some positive inspiration at the moment.'

'It is a simple sentiment, Rupert, but I believe in it: "Regrets are a waste of time; they are the past, now crippling you in the present. It is up to you whether you let them follow you into the future."'

'Wow! Those words are powerful, Boss.'

'Yes, they are, Rupert. Before you go back to the Waiting Zone, have you considered my offer? I must add that Sydney would be able to join you in the penthouse quarters as your forever-united-for-all-eternity partner.'

'Syd? What? I am so confused right now, Boss … can I think it all over and get back to you?'

'Yes, I understand. Of course, Rupert, take your time. I shall prepare the Vortex.'

Chapter Nineteen

Happily Ever After

I arrive back in dispatch, much to Harry's shock. I have never seen him so shaken up. Actually, I have never seen him shaken up; as I've already mentioned, he is always completely calm.

'What's going on, Rupert? Did I not send you right?'

'No, Harry, nothing like that. I'm just back, is all.'

'I will never understand you, lad! Here I thought that you'd waited all these years to get to Heaven – and what do you do? You turn right around and come back!'

'Yes, Harry. And it looks like it will be for eternity. Sorry – I must dash. See you later.'

I run off down the hall, nearly giving Jayden a heart attack as I pass dispatch. I run as fast as my legs will carry me. Everyone stops what they are doing, as they wonder why I am back. I suspect they are still feeling the after-effects of the night before.

I finally reach Syd's quarters, and I continuously bang on the door – rather loudly, I might add, to make certain she hears. She comes storming out, ready to give the person banging on her door quite a mouthful. However, as soon as she sees it is me, her whole attitude changes. She beams me a bright smile, wrapping her arms tightly around me, as if to say that she is never going to let me go again.

'What are you still doing here, Roo? I thought you left hours ago.'

'I did … I'm back.'

'Don't be silly! You can't come back …'

'Oh, Sydney, my dearest … apparently, I can … and I have.'

Her head shoots up, and her eyes narrow as she peers into my face. 'What's going on, Rupert?'

'Can I come in and tell you?'

We go in to her lounge. Yes, sure enough, Cupid is pointing in my direction, as usual. But this time, I don't mind; I want his arrow to strike – in fact, I do believe it struck a long time ago.

'Boss wants me to take over his job, which means I would remain in the Waiting Zone for all eternity. I will have my eternal happiness right here, Syd.'

Syd gazes at me for a moment. 'This doesn't make sense, Roo! What about Josie?'

'Brace yourself, Syd: Josie never died, and neither did our baby.' I pause for a moment to let that part sink in, and then I tell her the rest. 'Syd … Siobhan is my daughter, and Rosie is Josie.'

'Hold on a minute, Roo … I can't keep up. I just need to get this right in my head. There was no-one waiting for you at the gate, so you decided to come back to me as your second choice, is that it?'

She moves away and I see tears in her eyes.

'No, Syd, it is not like that at all! Do you not understand? For years, I have suppressed my true feelings for you; I felt that my loyalty had to be towards my wife and child. I believed I had to remain in the Waiting Zone to earn eternal happiness because I had taken my own life, but that they would be waiting for me when I earned my right to enter Heaven. I believed the three of us would spend eternity together – that my destined eternal happiness was with Josie and our child. Now I know that this has not been the case, and it never was. I am free of the shackles of my loyalty to them, as I realise that they are fine without me. My Earthly destiny with them is closed, through the power of my gift's release to Siobhan. Now I am free to love you for eternity, and that is what my eternal destiny has been all along. I promise I will do all in my power to ensure that we have eternal happiness. Syd – will you marry me?'

'Yes, Roo, I will marry you!'

Epilogue

So, we did exactly that. I contacted Boss to accept his job, and so he was able to move on to his eternal happiness. On the same day as my inauguration as Boss of the Waiting Zone, I married Syd. It was the best day ever. She has always been my soulmate – we have been destined to be together for all eternity. I can see clearly now that this is why we were such good friends for so long. Syd and I just 'get each other'; we always have and always will. Now, after thirty-four years of friendship, we join together as one to share eternity; we don't need to go to Heaven to have eternal happiness – we have it right here. As I watch her walk up the aisle, wearing the most beautiful, sparkling-white dress I have ever seen, I know that this is it: the final piece of my jigsaw is in place, and I am now complete.

As Syd has decided to stay in the Waiting Zone with me as my wife for all eternity, she has signed away her desire to enter Heaven, thus giving me the power over her gift. Just as the Boss decided the destination of where my gift should end up, I, as the new Boss, have control of this miracle. I decide to keep Syd's gift right here for us.

Our little miracle will bring wonderment to our lives, lasting for all eternity. I can't wait to see Syd's face when she discovers it! She has always craved children, and to think that she has given herself this treasured gift – for she alone supplied the gift, and I have just navigated it in the right direction, as I now have the power to do so.

Syd's and my time of eternal happiness commences, and the next chapter now begins for each of us – and for the two of us together, and for the precious one that we will have …

Acknowledgements

This book would not exist without the loving, positive support I received from my dear friends, Sascha and Donna, at buildingbeautifulbonds.com. You are amazing and inspiring women! I am so blessed to have you in my life.

Nyanda, thank you for your positive review at a critical point during the process.

To hubby, thank you for my learning and for your love.

To my children Dylan, Eithen, Kiera, Saoirse, Eimear and Mary – you are my inspiration and my passion. My heart glows for you all every day.

Mum and Dad, my sisters Emma and Lisa, my brothers Jonathan, Mathew and Luke, my Aunty Paddy, and my entire family and friends – thanks to all of you for always believing in me. I would not be who I am today if you were not part of my life.

Tesha, the way my book has touched your heart has affirmed that I am on the right path. Thank you for being wonderful.

Finally, Bill and Bev, thank you for gracing my life with your presence, you are very special people.

Life is good to me.

About the Author

Karen McDermott currently resides in Perth, Western Australia, with her husband and six children, after emigrating from Ireland in September 2008. Her children are the most important things in her life. Writing and publishing come a close second.

She came from Ireland – a place of magical beauty – and she now resides in Australia – a place of inspiration and opportunity; these two special but very different places, together, give her the passion and determination necessary to incorporate positive writing in her life daily.

Karen successfully completed a diploma in humanities, which instilled in her a desire for learning new things; this, combined with the experience of a miscarriage, led her to write this book in order to give hope and a degree of understanding to women who suffer such pain.

Karen has had many successes in life and writing is one she is proud of.

'From all negative situations is the potential for a positive outcome.'

Find out more about Karen at:

mmhpress.com

karenmcdermott.com.au

Readers' Messages to the Author

This one experience really seemed to lack any positive side; although everyone around assured you 'it happened for a reason', which might have soothed your logic mind, somehow your heart still yearned for a deeper kind of understanding.

The Visitor gave me the answer my heart longed for.

My own experience with miscarriage now has a whole new meaning which I am able to positively accept and embrace.

The deeper sense of understanding that I have gained from reading this fantastic book, lovingly created from another woman's similar personal experience, relates not only to miscarriage itself but also to many circumstances that I have experienced – and will go on to experience in my life. Thank you for the insights shared, Karen.

With love from,

Donna Di Lallo

The Visitor is captivating, humorous and heart-rending. McDermott translates beautifully a topic traditionally shrouded in silence. It is a true privilege to partake in her spiritual journey.

McDermott is the true gift!

Sascha Brooks

Also by K P Weaver

The Enlightenment Series

The Visitor

The Wish Giver

The Memory Taker

The Life Magic Series

The Power of Knowing

The Magic of Mindfulness

The Miracle of Intent

www.ingramcontent.com/pod-product-compliance
Lightning Source LLC
Chambersburg PA
CBHW010750310726
48980CB00003B/371
9780645520552